The girlfriend's enemy approaches . . .

"I don't bite," Kylie called down to him from the lifeguard chair.

"That's not what I heard." Johnny regretted it the second it was out of his mouth. Why did he say that? He climbed up and sat down next to her, careful to keep his elbows at a reasonable distance. "Sorry, Kylie. I don't know why I said that."

"I do," she said, glancing at him before turning her attention to the beach. "It's because your girlfriend can't stand me."

"But it's mutual, so . . ."

"Not really." She grabbed her sunblock and squeezed a glob on her arm. Johnny watched her rub it in, then do the same with her other arm. "I mean, I don't like Jane. But I don't *hate* her. I've tried a couple of times to get her to talk about it, just forget it after all these years, but she told me to get out of her face. So I did."

It. The famous *it*. The *it* that Jane never wanted to talk about, yet referred to every time they passed Kylie in the hall at school or saw her at the mall. He didn't even know what the *it* was.

But he had a feeling that by summer's end, he'd find out much more than that.

Brothers Trilogy

Johnny

ZOE ZIMMERMAN

BANTAM BOOKS
NEW YORK · TORONTO · LONDON · SYDNEY · AUCKLAND

RL: 6, AGES 012 AND UP

JOHNNY

A Bantam Book / July 2000

Cover photography by Michael Segal.

Produced by 17th Street Productions,
an Alloy Online, Inc. company.
33 West 17th Street
New York, NY 10011.

ISBN: 0-553-49324-8

Visit us on the Web! www.randomhouse.com/teens

Published simultaneously in the United States and Canada

Bantam Books is an imprint of Random House Children's Books, a
division of Random House, Inc. BANTAM BOOKS and the rooster
colophon are registered trademarks of Random House, Inc. Bantam Books,
1540 Broadway, New York, New York 10036.

PRINTED IN THE UNITED STATES OF AMERICA

OPM   0 9 8 7 6 5 4 3 2 1

One

*J*UST A WEEK *till Jane arrives,* seventeen-year-old Johnny Ford thought as he eyed the beach full of bathing beauties. *One week, and the girl I'm actually allowed to gawk at will be here.*

He couldn't wait to see his girlfriend in a bikini—*and* to have someone on his wavelength to talk to. He'd been stuck living in a pit of an apartment on the boardwalk of Surf City, California, for two months now with his younger brothers. He loved the knuckleheads, but they'd been driving him crazy since day one back in June. Sixteen-year-old Danny and fifteen-year-old Kevin simply didn't understand the word *responsibility.* They thought life was about having fun. Johnny had been trying to disabuse them of that very wrong notion—without results. Right now Danny and Kevin, who he'd parted ways with moments ago at the employees' entrance to the Surf City Resort Hotel, were probably kissing their own girlfriends behind the storage shed with one eye open for the boss.

Johnny smiled and shook his head as he slung his knapsack higher over his shoulder and headed for said storage shed between the pool area and the path to the hotel's private beach. No knuckleheads kissing. Good. That probably meant they were already up by the pool, fetching towels and refilling glasses of iced tea—like the good cabana boys they were.

Johnny took a moment to raise his face to the sun. Life was good. There was nothing quite like morning sunshine and an ocean breeze in August. It was one of those perfect days, postcardlike. The kind of day where everything went right.

"Omigod," he heard a girl shriek in horror. "We're wearing the *same* bikini!"

"Well, *I'm* not changing!" shrieked a higher-pitched voice (if that was possible). "*You* change!"

Johnny rolled his eyes. Just your average conversation on the grounds of the ultraexclusive Surf City Resort Hotel. Which reminded him it was time to get moving.

He opened the storage shed, which was a squat structure nestled back amid some foliage and palm trees. Inside were the basics of his job as a lifeguard: various signal flags, a first-aid kit the size of a toolbox, a fleet of fully charged walkie-talkies, a bullhorn, and the fluorescent orange flotation pod that Johnny liked to call Excalibur—like King Arthur's sword. He'd heard other lifeguards call it different things. Excalibur was the primary tool of

2

the beach lifeguard. It was about two feet long, had a pair of molded handles on either side, was made of hard plastic, and spent most of its time attached by a rope to Johnny's wrist. It had many uses. Life preserver. Signal beacon (it could be seen immediately in the water from the air). Even self-defense tool. Like a Jedi with a light saber, Johnny didn't leave home without it. No lifeguard was to ever go anywhere without one while on duty. Cardinal rule *numero uno*.

He grabbed a walkie-talkie, a bullhorn, and an Excalibur and headed for the high, white lifeguard chair that overlooked his stretch of beach. The early morning brought surfers and belly boarders, but they were out there on their own. They usually cleared out without being told since Johnny's stretch of beach was private and owned by the hotel.

But one of them was sitting in his chair. A girl. Her back was to him; she sat ramrod straight. Her blond ponytail moved left, then straight, then right. Then again and again and again. So she was playing lifeguard, huh? Not cool.

Man, he hated confrontations. Now he'd have to tell surfer chick to beat it. It was dangerous for someone to pose as a lifeguard by sitting up there. Swimmers would feel safer thinking they were being watched, which meant they might swim out farther than they should. And what would surfer girl do then, huh? Apologize while they panicked at how far out they'd ended up?

As Johnny neared the chair, he called up, "Excuse me. Hey—that chair is for lifeguards only. You'll have to—"

Johnny stopped dead when the girl turned to face him.

"Hi, Johnny." She beamed a smile at him.

Johnny gulped, trying to keep cool on the outside. Kylie Smith. Fellow lifeguard. And *more*.

He hadn't recognized her from the back. But then again, why would he? He'd never paid Kylie much attention, for good reason. Back in June, during lifeguard training sessions, he'd spotted her running around in her regulation one-piece, blue Surf City bathing suit. For half a minute they'd even been named partners, but the boss had changed his mind and assigned Kylie way down the beach before they'd even gotten a chance to shake hands. Johnny had been *very, very* relieved. He'd seen Kylie here and there a few times over the summer. The only reason he'd noticed her at all was because she went to his high school, Spring Valley, and she'd graduated this past June, same as him.

Oh, and plus the fact that she was evil and horrible.

Well, at least according to Jane. Kylie Smith and Jane Jarvis were enemies. They hated each other's guts.

She sure doesn't look evil, Johnny thought as he shot Kylie a weak smile. Honey blond hair waving to her shoulders, blue-green eyes. Petite. Sweet looking, in an angelic sort of way. Maybe it was the sweetest-looking girls who were the most evil.

Johnny wouldn't know. He'd been with Jane

for a long time—three years. She was his only point of reference.

Kylie climbed down from the chair and smiled at him, her blue-green eyes bright.

Man, she has a nice body, he thought. *Hey, now!* his inner voice piped up. *Let's get that thought right out of here, bud.*

He couldn't help but notice the smattering of freckles across her nose that scrunched up when she squinted in the sunlight. Did evil ogres have freckles? Johnny didn't think so. A pair of sunglasses and a lifeguard whistle hung from her long, tanned neck. A waterproof diver's watch was strapped to her left wrist. Johnny also noticed a tattooed ring of dolphins circling her right ankle.

What's with all these girls and tattoos? he wondered. He'd have to ask Raven, Danny's girlfriend. She was the tattoo queen. Personally, Johnny thought tattoos were ugly. If nature didn't put it there, it didn't belong there. That was one of his mottoes. According to Kevin, Johnny had one too many mottoes. The kid thought Johnny should learn to go with the flow. Like he'd take advice from a fifteen-year-old. Please.

Johnny tossed his gear up on the chair and leaned against it. "Lost?" he asked, instantly regretting both the lame joke and the snide tone to his voice.

"Nope," she said, stretching her tanned, toned arms over her head. "Beach asked me to meet him here. He's supposed to assign me to a new chair today."

"Oh." Beach McGriff was Johnny's boss—was *every* lifeguard's boss in Surf City (even the ones like Johnny who watched over the private beaches).

"So I figured since I was here early, I might as well watch over the kids who were swimming," she added.

Johnny nodded. He wished kids' parents wouldn't let them swim before the lifeguards came on duty at 9:30 A.M. But a mess of kids were always playing in the water when Johnny arrived.

He glanced at his watch and scanned the beach for his partner, Drew. Nowhere to be found. As usual. "Uh, Kylie, since you're here and waiting, would you mind helping me plant the flags?"

"Sure," she said with a smile, following him to the shed. "Hey, so where's Drew? Isn't he supposed to get here fifteen minutes before you to set up?"

"*Supposed to* being the key phrase," Johnny replied. Drew was an assistant lifeguard who floated around to help out on particularly crowded stretches of beach, like Johnny's. August was prime season at Surf City, and the beach was already crowded before its official opening time of 10 A.M. Johnny needed a *real* partner. When Beach got here, Johnny was going to let loose on what a lazy screwup Drew had been the past month. "But we *are* talking about a kid who spends more time checking out girls than the water."

Kylie laughed—a warm, melodic sound that surprised Johnny. *Did you expect her to laugh like the Wicked Witch of the West or something?* he wondered. *Yeah, I think maybe I did.*

6

Kylie opened the shed and dragged out some red flags. "I think this is the most conversation we've ever had, considering we went to the same high school for four years."

Johnny glanced at her, surprised again. He hadn't expected her to say that. Or *anything* concerning the fact that they hadn't said more than three words to each other in high school. Johnny had once said *excuse me* when she'd been unknowingly blocking his path to the library. She'd said sorry and turned to look at him, and they'd locked eyes for a moment. There had been a forbidden quality to that moment; it was a feeling Johnny had never forgotten. There was something very black and white about the forbidden—no gray areas. When your girlfriend hated someone, you didn't chat with the person about homework or student-council elections. You just didn't. And Johnny believed in stuff like that. The easy difference between right and wrong.

"Yeah, um, so . . ." *Good, John. Very articulate,* he chastised himself mentally. But he wasn't supposed to even be talking to her, was he? Wasn't he betraying Jane by standing so close to the girl? Johnny stepped away as he pulled out the rest of the flags.

"So, how's your summer been?" she asked as they began walking back toward the lifeguard station, their arms full of flags.

He glanced at her. "Well, my brothers and I are a team in the volleyball tournament next week, so I've basically spent the entire summer worrying about it."

The Surf City volleyball tournament, sponsored by Fizz Cola and held at the hotel, was *everything* to Johnny. If the Fords won, they would pocket ten thousand dollars in cash—an invaluable chunk of change now that Johnny was off to Allman College in three weeks. He and his brothers had been practicing all summer, but they'd been training extra hard lately. In a little over a week Johnny would know whether he'd have to get one job or five to put himself through school.

"I'm so psyched about the tournament," Kylie said. "I love volleyball. I mean, I'm not a big-time player, but I've always loved joining a game on the beach."

Johnny sneaked a peek at her. So she liked volleyball, huh?

"I saw you play a bunch of times at Spring Valley," she continued. "The team's lost a real star now that you've graduated."

Johnny felt his cheeks redden at the compliment. "Thanks," he said, kicking up some sand. He knew Kylie had been on the swim team at SV High, but he'd only seen one meet. Without knowing she was on the team, Johnny and a couple of friends had gone to cheer them on after volleyball practice. Jane had heard he was there and flipped out.

"And I've seen you and your brothers practice too," Kylie added. "My two roommates and I were walking around one evening after work and saw a bunch of the teams practicing. I have to say, Johnny—you guys are awesome."

Could you stop being so nice! Johnny wanted to yell

at her. *I'm supposed to hate you by association.*

But instead Johnny found himself grinning. *Don't ask her who she's rooming with,* he told himself. *Don't ask her where she lives. Don't ask her anything personal.*

"So, um, is Jane coming down to watch you guys win?" Kylie asked.

Johnny froze for a second. She'd surprised him again. He hadn't figured she'd bring up Jane directly. Nor had he expected she'd be so positive about him and his brothers *winning.* That had been a cool touch.

"Uh, yeah, she's supposed to arrive in a week," Johnny said as they reached the lifeguard chair. "I can't wait till she gets here. I haven't seen her in—"

What am I doing? Johnny wondered. *Kylie doesn't need to hear how much I'm dying to see the girl she hates. Just shut up and set up the flags.*

Kylie tilted her head at him but then took some flags and planted them about seventy-five feet on one side of the chair while Johnny took care of the other side. All bathers had to stay inside the flags so it was easier for the guards to keep watch over them. If they swam outside the flags or went out too far, they risked getting whistled in.

"So what's it like working the high-end beach?" Kylie asked, and he was relieved she'd changed the subject. "Do you find gold watches and rolls of hundreds left on the sand at the end of the day?"

Johnny laughed and untangled a flag so it would blow free in the wind. "I wish. But nope, just the same old soda cans and hamburger wrappers and empty suntan lotion bottles and—"

He was interrupted by the whirring motor of a dune buggy. Johnny and Kylie turned around. Beach McGriff. When he wasn't taking a quick shift in a lifeguard chair, Beach was riding up and down the Surf City beaches on his ATV, looking for trouble. To *stop* it, not make it.

"Hey, kids," Beach called out as he stopped the buggy by the station. "Kylie, I know you're probably thinking you hit the jackpot with your new post, but trust me, you didn't. You gotta work with Johnny here, Mr. Serious. Plus just because this is the ritziest stretch of beach doesn't mean the chair comes with air-conditioning. Sorry."

Beach cracked up at his own sorry humor, but Johnny and Kylie stared at each other in total confusion.

"Uh, Beach," Johnny began.

"Yeah, Beach—," Kylie said.

Beach cranked the engine on his ATV and revved. Johnny stepped forward and put a hand on Beach's arm. "What are you talking about?" he yelled over the engine.

Beach put a hand up to his ear. "Speak up and make it quick, Ford. Gotta motor." He cracked up again in laughter. "Get it—*gotta motor. Motor.*" He revved again to make his point, chuckling away.

"What . . . are . . . you . . . talking . . . about?" Johnny yelled.

Beach hooked a thumb at Kylie. "She's your new partner!" The boss turned to Kylie. "Smith, you were

10

supposed to be assigned to the next stretch, but Drew begged for a transfer, so I switched you two. Said Johnny was always on his case and torturing him out of a summer. I figured you two would make a great team, considering you're the only lifeguard who has the guts to tell Ford here to go jump in the ocean." Beach turned back to Johnny. "Ford, word of advice: Lighten up. Summer's almost over. *Enjoy* it."

Johnny could tell Kylie was trying not to laugh. He was about to defend himself to Beach, but the guy roared away in a dusting of spun-up sand. Johnny covered his eyes, wondering what he did to deserve this. "Oh, so maybe I should just let someone drown while I'm rubbing suntan lotion on my chest to attract the babes to the mighty lifeguard!" Johnny yelled over the roar, but Beach was gone.

"It would definitely work," Kylie said, climbing up to the chair.

He glanced at her. She had on a straight face, and she wasn't even looking at him. She was staring out at the ocean, doing her job already.

But he'd caught what she'd meant.

Or was he being conceited? Maybe she'd meant *they'd definitely work out* as partners.

Yeah.

And maybe his girlfriend wouldn't go postal when she heard they *were* partners.

A half hour later Johnny realized he'd exhausted all his reasons for avoiding the chair. He'd made a thousand excuses for why he couldn't join her yet.

11

Had to warn two kids who kept swimming too far. Had to ask a bunch of girls to turn down their boom box. Had to patrol their stretch of surf in both directions. Had to make sure the red flags were dug into the sand okay . . .

"I don't bite," Kylie called down to him.

Johnny looked up at her. "That's not what I heard."

He mentally shook his head, regretting it the second it was out of his mouth. Why did he say that?

Sighing, Johnny climbed up and sat down next to her, careful to keep his elbows at a reasonable distance. "Sorry, Kylie. I don't know why I said that."

"I do," she said, glancing at him before turning her attention to the beach. "It's because your girlfriend can't stand me."

Kylie sure is direct, isn't she? Johnny thought.

"I guess," he said, aware that it was refreshing and appealing to simply speak the truth. "But it's mutual, so . . ."

"Not really," she said, grabbing her sunblock and squeezing a glob on her arm. Johnny watched her rub it in, then do the same with her other arm. "I mean, I don't like Jane. I haven't since . . . well, I don't like her. But I don't *hate* her. I've tried a couple of times to get her to talk about it, just forget it after all these years, but she told me to get out of her face. So I did."

It. The famous it. The it that Jane never wanted to talk about, yet referred to every time they passed Kylie in the hall at school or saw her at the mall. He didn't even know what the *it* was.

Anyway, who cared? Kylie had already told him more than he wanted to know just now. Dying to change the subject, Johnny said, "So, um, welcome to the hotel beach."

Kylie smiled. "Too intense a convo for ten A.M., huh?"

Johnny couldn't help but smile. *Yes, indeed it was,* he thought. The warm scent of her cocoa butter reached his nose. He loved that smell. It reminded him of all things summer and beach. Of sunshine and swimming and glistening skin . . .

"We don't have to talk, Johnny," Kylie suddenly added. "If you feel uncomfortable about it. I know this is weird for both of us. So, why don't we just do our jobs, and if one of us wants to say something, like, 'Hey, look at that kid without a bathing suit,' or, 'Nice day, isn't it?' or, 'How should we get our revenge on Beach McGriff?' we will."

Johnny turned to her, unable to tone down the smile on his face. This Kylie Smith was one okay girl. He stuck out his hand. "Deal, partner."

Kylie took his hand and shook it. Her hand was soft.

He turned back to the water, sat back, and focused on his job. Kylie did the same.

By noon the surf was dotted with swimmers. The beach around them had quickly filled up with hotel guests, beach umbrellas, and waiters delivering drinks. Johnny kept count of the people in the water. He whistled two kids back between the flags. But overall, it was a slow day. No radio chatter. No riptide warnings. Plenty of sunshine cut by a cool breeze off the water. And not much reason to make small talk—or real talk.

Two attractive girls in bikinis—one blonde, one brunette—strolled in front of the chair, sloppily hiding the fact that they were scoping Johnny. They glanced at him out of the corners of their eyes, sneaked looks over their shoulders, and giggled.

"You're quite a girl magnet," Kylie said. "They're the fifth or sixth group to come by and gawk at you."

It was the first words between them in two hours.

Johnny chuckled, thankful for the tension break. "I'm taken, remember?"

"How could I forget?" Kylie said, punching him on the arm.

Johnny turned to face her, once again surprised by her good humor. "Besides, I'm on duty."

Whoa. Now what was he doing? He was *flirting,* that's what. *Good going, John. Flirt with the girlfriend's enemy.*

"Oh, *besides,*" she said, staring out at the water.

Huh? What happened? He'd been joking, something he thought she'd appreciate, like a truce. So why did she seem upset?

"So, you're saying that if you *weren't* on duty," Kylie began, "you'd be flirting up a storm with any of the girls who've hit on you this morning?"

"I—"

Kylie bolted up on the platform. "Your girlfriend and I might not be friends, Johnny, but that doesn't mean I haven't admired the fact that she's had a serious boyfriend for three years. Everyone at Spring Valley felt that way. Every day some couple would break up after five minutes or two months or whatever, but there you'd guys be, together, always. It made people feel like it was possible—"

"So you're angry at me on Jane's behalf?" he interrupted with a soft smile.

"No," she whispered as she sat back down. "I'm angry at you on my *own* behalf."

Ah. Now he got it. "Because of what it means, right? That even a guy who seems totally true blue might cheat."

Kylie nodded and smoothed a stray strand of hair back into her ponytail.

"I think you should know something, Kylie."

She turned to face him. "What?"

"I was joking."

"Oh," she said, shooting him a weak smile. She glanced at him, then back at the water.

Interesting. Kylie wasn't some cold, evil, heartless drama queen who plotted the downfall of rivals she didn't even have yet. In fact, she seemed so compassionate, so concerned, so . . . dare he think it? *Nice*.

"What was it that happened between you and Jane?" he asked.

"You don't know?" Kylie was clearly surprised. "I figured she'd told you every detail of how evil I am a long time ago."

Johnny shook his head.

"It's a long story," she said. "A stupid story about cheerleading and some guy, and you really don't want to hear about it."

"Sure, I do," Johnny prodded.

Kylie gnawed her lower lip. "Jane and I were

15

friends . . . Everything just blew up bigger than it should have. But everything does when you're in seventh grade. We just stopped talking and never started again. Pretty cut-and-dried."

"That's about as much detail as I got from Jane," Johnny said. "I don't even bring it up anymore."

"So, now you can tell *me* something," Kylie said. "Why isn't Jane spending the summer with you here?"

"She's working as a counselor at a sleep-away camp near Spring Valley," Johnny explained. "Her parents begged her since her bratty kid brother goes there. And she hates the beach anyway. She's a mountains girl."

"The mountains are great and all, but I couldn't imagine hating the beach," Kylie said.

Me either, Johnny thought. "Plus she knew I'd be so busy with the job and volleyball that we wouldn't have spent much time together anyway." He chuckled uneasily. Somehow that came out as if he was defending their couplehood. "We're treating the summer as a dry run for college since we'll be at different schools. It'll get us used to staying together while we're apart."

Kylie nodded. "Where are you two going?"

"Jane's going to Floyd University in San Diego," Johnny replied. "I'll be up in San Francisco at Allman College."

"No way!" Kylie exclaimed. "I'm going to Allman too!"

Johnny gulped. "Say *what?*"

If Johnny wasn't so tan, he'd have turned white.

TWO

T HE ELECTRONIC BLURP that was the phone echoed from somewhere inside the Ford brothers' apartment on the Surf City boardwalk. It stopped as suddenly as it rang.

"Johnnnyyy!" Danny Ford's voice boomed from one of the bedrooms, a dull roar over the pulse of loud music. "Phooonnne! It's Jannne!"

Johnny smiled and shot up, searching for the cordless. "Danny, where's the phone?" Danny and Raven were listening to a bootleg tape of some band they were heading out to see live tonight. Johnny forgot the name . . . the Funeral Homeys or Obi-Wannabes or something like that.

"No clue, dude," came Danny's muffled reply. "Kevin was yapping at Penny on the phone in the kitchen. Ask him."

Johnny rolled his eyes; Kevin had left to meet Penny a half hour ago. The cordless was nowhere to be found, and Jane was calling long distance. Johnny rushed into the kitchen—success! The phone, smeared with jelly and toast crumbs, was on the counter. He shook his head and grabbed a paper towel to wipe it off, then clicked it on. "Danny, hang up. I've got it! Hello?"

"Johnny?"

At the sound of Jane's voice Johnny suddenly froze.

Was he supposed to tell her Kylie was his new partner? Back in June he'd casually mentioned that Jane was life guarding at Surf City but that she worked a mile down the resort from him. Jane hadn't been pleased to know her enemy was his coworker, even with all that beach separating them. How would she react to knowing they were sharing a *chair?*

Or, um, a *college?*

"Hi, sweetheart," he said. "How's it going?"

"Everything's good," she said. "And everything'll be great when I see you."

Johnny smiled. "Pacific Coach number sixty-six, gate twelve, Friday morning, seven short days from today. I leave anything out?"

Jane laughed. "Is there anyone more reliable than you? Oh, wait—you *did* leave something out. How much you miss me."

Johnny's smile widened. "Oh. That. Didn't even cross my mind."

"Johnny!"

"Okay, okay. I miss you. I miss you a lot. I'm

just so used to torturing my brothers that I do it to everyone out of habit now."

Jane sighed. "Hope you haven't picked up any of their habits."

"Just the bad ones," he replied, kicking an empty Pop-Tarts box aside as he headed back into the living room. "Imagine what college will be like. I'll be totally wrecked by the end of one semester." Johnny dropped down in the reclining chair and rested his head against the pillow.

"Don't bring that up," Jane said, and Johnny instantly regretted saying anything. He kept remembering that college was less than a month away, but he kept forgetting that he and Jane would be a long ways apart.

"Sorry," he said softly. "But we shouldn't just dodge the fact that we're going to separate schools. It's gonna be happening sooner rather than later."

There was a pause on Jane's end. "I know," she finally said. "That doesn't mean I have to like it."

"So we'll have a great time next weekend," Johnny promised. "Me and the bros will finally get to kick butt in the volleyball tournament, then you and I can spend the last week of the summer together. It'll be great."

"I know," Jane replied, her tone improving. "I can't wait."

"So your parents are okay with you staying with me?" he asked.

"Totally," she said. "We shouldn't have worried. My father told me he trusts you completely. He thinks you're more responsible than he is. Plus I have a feeling my mom told my dad that we decided to wait. . . ."

"Wait for what?" he asked, relieved that her folks hadn't insisted she stay at a hotel.

"For *you know,*" she said. "Till we're *older.*"

Oh. That. Jane had made it clear they weren't doing *anything* till they graduated from high school and were in college. She was probably more conservative than her parents could have dreamed. Which was fine by Johnny. Yeah, he was very, very attracted to Jane. And sometimes he wished they could just—

But sex wasn't everything. Or maybe he and Jane had been a couple for so long that Johnny had simply learned not to expect anything more than making out. Once he and Jane were in college and visited each other, maybe things would seem different. Maybe they'd seem like adults. A few of his friends back home had lost their virginity already, but a few others, like Johnny, hadn't. It really wasn't the big deal movies and TV made it out to be. Some people bragged about having sex; some people didn't talk about it one way or the other. But he didn't feel any pressure to finally do it.

"Your brothers don't mind that I'll be staying there?" Jane asked, cutting into his thoughts.

Just then the music from Danny's room cut off. "They don't have a choice. I've been putting up with their romances all summer. So they can deal with mine for a while."

"*You're* the one who has to deal with her," came

20

Danny's voice as he and Raven emerged from his room. "I just live here."

"What did he say?" Jane asked.

Johnny shot deadly lasers from his eyes "Nothing. Danny was talking to his girlfriend."

Raven, dressed in her usual skate-girl tattered clothing, grinned at him.

"So, um, Jane," Johnny began. He had to tell her about Kylie. If he didn't mention it, she'd be furious when she found out for herself. "There's something—"

"Steve and Ben, you stop that right now!" Jane shrieked, interrupting him. "Johnny—I have to go. Two of my kids are pelting each other with chocolate-chip cookies. That's it! No cookies for your bedtime snack! And no dessert at lunch to-morrow for either of you! I said stop it! Johnny, I'll call you tomorrow—I miss you, bye!"

"Bye," he said into the dial tone. *Oh and before you go, guess who my new partner is? The girl you've hated since seventh grade,* he added mentally. Johnny clicked off the phone and set it on the arm of the recliner. *And guess what, we're going to the same college too.*

"You look pretty sad for a guy whose girlfriend is coming to visit next weekend," Danny com-mented, gnawing on a pretzel stick.

Johnny slumped back and stared at the ball game on the tube. "It's not the good-byes on the phone, dude. It's the good-bye coming up. The one when we go our separate ways in September."

"What do you mean?" Raven asked, dropping

down on the sofa. The pink streaks in her hair never failed to startle Johnny. "You guys are splitting up?"

"Are you kidding?" Danny interrupted. "Johnny and Jane? Class Couple at Spring Valley High? No chance. They've been together since, what, *ninth* grade?"

"The summer *after* ninth," Johnny corrected.

"Wow, that's three whole years," Raven said with a gleam in her eyes. "So you've never kissed another girl except Jane?"

"I kissed plenty of girls before Jane," Johnny snapped. Which was true. Johnny had been something of the class heartthrob until Jane had caught his eye . . . and his heart. They'd been the only two people who actually liked earth science and math. They'd thought the same things were stupid. They'd spent hours walking up and down the hills in their neighborhood. They'd talked about serious things. Jane had never once told Johnny he was too serious or too responsible, the way other people always did. Like him, she thought responsibility was a trait to *admire*.

Raven snatched a pretzel stick from Danny and bit off the end. "So why do you look so unhappy?"

"We're going to different colleges," Johnny explained, picking up a volleyball and tossing it up in the air over and over. "I'll be in the Bay Area. She'll be in San Diego. Which is . . . let's put it this way: She might as well be in New York."

"But you still plan to stay together," Raven noted. Johnny nodded. "Of course."

"Yeah, right," Danny scoffed. "Johnny 'Faithful' Ford. We'll see how long that lasts once you get an invite to that first sorority mixer."

Johnny threw a pillow—hard—at Danny. "Jane and I have had all summer to get used to being apart. We'll see each other on breaks and for long weekends. It'll work."

Danny laughed.

"Give the guy a break, Dan," Raven protested. "It's going to be hard enough as it is. I think it's great that they're trying to make it work."

Danny rolled his eyes, then stood up. "Once Johnny sees what else exists, trust me, he'll forget about Jane 'I Don't Have a Sense of Humor' Jarvis."

Johnny glared at Danny. "Watch it. That's my girlfriend you're talking about."

"Johnny's had all summer to see what else 'exists,'" Raven pointed out. "He hasn't cheated on Jane yet, so why would he at college?"

"Because he won't be distracted by the *tourney* in September," Danny explained. "Or his two troublemaker brothers."

Johnny groaned. "Don't you two have a concert to get to?"

Danny looked at his watch. "Hey, Rave. He's right. We've gotta go."

Of course, I'm right, Johnny thought. *I'm always right.*

Just once, I'd like to know what it feels like to be Danny or Kevin. To go with the flow. To rely on other people to tell you where you're supposed to be and when. To not worry . . . about anything.

Raven stood up. "Smile, Johnny. At least she's coming to see you next weekend."

Johnny nodded. Then the door slammed, and they were gone. Johnny sighed and upped the volume on the ball game.

Danny's lucky to have Raven, he thought. *Hope he doesn't mess it up.*

Knucklehead Number 1 did have a good point, though. Johnny and Jane had made it fine through the summer because Johnny *did* have a one-track mind: the volleyball tournament. He'd spent every moment of his spare time practicing. And on top of v-ball, his brothers' misadventures in romance *had* kept Johnny suitably stressed as well. There simply hadn't been room for anything but holding the team together for the tournament.

So what if the tourney didn't exist? he asked himself. *Would you have let your eye wander up and down the beach?* It wasn't as if Johnny hadn't had countless opportunities. Girls seemed to have a thing for lifeguards. As if there was anything sexy about a nose whited out by sunblock.

No. I love Jane, he reminded himself. *Always have. She's my girlfriend.* Plain and simple. Black and white. She was his girlfriend, and he loved her.

But Johnny could hear it in Jane's voice every time he talked with her. The time and distance were wearing on her. The frustration came through loud and clear even though the words were never spoken. *Could* their relationship survive separate colleges?

Better question was: Would their relationship

survive the fact that Kylie Smith was his partner when Jane found out?

The next morning at 6 A.M. sharp the Fords mounted their bikes and rode to a deserted stretch of beach where they'd set up their practice volleyball net. Danny and Kevin had complained bitterly when Johnny had insisted on the prework practice sessions for the month of August, but they'd come around to see they needed all the practice they could get.

"Oh, man, there's Jabba!" Danny said, laughing, pointing with one hand, and steering his bike with the other. "What a loser!"

Johnny eyed the big, bearded, bug-eyed man who was opening up Jabba's Palace, a greasy restaurant on the boardwalk. Jabba had fired Danny from his job as a waiter after Danny had told him off (even Johnny had later agreed Danny had been justified). But all worked out okay: Danny had landed a spot as a cabana boy at the hotel, the same job that Kevin had held all summer (and it certainly tickled Kevin to no end that he had seniority over his older bro). As cabana boys, Kevin and Danny hustled towels, served drinks, cleaned messes, and basically did a waiter's job at half the salary.

But at least they got to spend the day in the sunshine near a nice pool, Johnny figured. And Kevin was on the bonus plan: Being a cabana boy was how he'd met his girlfriend, Penny. She worked at the hotel as well, but her job was a little less defined and more secure since her father owned not just the farm, but the big kahuna, the ball of wax, the shooting match, and the whole enchilada too. The hotel was his kingdom.

Naturally, the old man hadn't smiled too brightly upon his daughter's infatuation with Kevin, a mere commoner in the court of the king. But Kevin had shown Penny's father a thing or two about earning respect. Austin Booth had been impressed. So had Johnny. He knew he was seeing his youngest brother literally grow up right before his eyes. Kevin and Penny had been an item ever since.

Way to go, little bro, Johnny thought.

He was jostled from his reverie as they biked past a beautiful blonde jogging in the other direction. All three Fords did a double take.

"Whoa," Danny muttered.

"Times two," Kevin added.

Johnny chuckled. "Easy, kids. We're all spoken for, remember?"

Johnny was used to seeing beautiful women in bikinis. All day, every day at work. Not that he was immune to the sight of a total babe. But he'd never let an amazing-looking girl distract him from his job. Life guarding—no matter what *Baywatch* jokes came to mind—demanded concentration and professionalism.

Anyway, just because he couldn't help looking every now and then didn't mean he'd ever *do* anything, like actually flirt back with the Heather Grahams of the beach or the Keri Russells who clapped as he whistled swimmers into submission.

26

He absolutely had been joking when he'd made that "besides, I'm on duty" comment to Kylie. Because at the end of the day, when the girls finally left him alone and he could once again stare out at the clear blue Pacific, Johnny knew he wanted to be with Jane.

He just wanted someone he could *talk* to. And that was Jane. Maybe she wasn't the most vivacious girl in the room. Maybe she wasn't the most scintillating. In fact, you could pile up a wall of adjectives that didn't apply to Jane: wild, dramatic, bubbly, seductive, yada, yada, yada. But Johnny loved Jane because he found she was most like himself. Low-key. Smart. Sometimes funny. Always faithful. And always serious.

He wondered what really happened between Jane and Kylie back in seventh grade. It was hard to imagine no-nonsense Jane holding a five-year grudge over something to do with cheerleading and a guy.

When the Fords reached their destination, they got off their bikes and wheeled them down the path to the beach. Maybe later this morning Kylie would elaborate on what the big beef was all about. She'd talked his ear off yesterday afternoon. All about her expectations for Allman, how psyched she was, about her family, her favorite teachers at Spring Valley, funny stories about her dog. The girl could sure talk. In an entertaining way too. Johnny wasn't used to that. He was a guy of few words, and Jane was the girl version.

Johnny had been sort of distracted yesterday afternoon by the fact that he wasn't supposed to be talking to Kylie, let alone *enjoying* her company. But she was so pleasant, and she told a lot of jokes without even trying. He could have worse partners, like no-show Drew or Paul Breyer, the egomaniac lifeguard who worked a few stretches of beach over from Johnny. Paul looked like a young Brad Pitt and claimed he was the lead singer in a five-guy band like 'N Sync back home that was poised for superstardom.

I'm lucky to have Kylie as a partner, he thought as he and his brothers dropped their bikes under the trees near their net.

"What's with you, man?" Kevin asked, squinting at him.

"Yeah, John," Danny added. "You're too quiet. You didn't even bug out about me dropping my bike on yours."

"Huh?" Johnny said.

"Oh, man!" Kevin said. "Something is up!"

I'm gonna regret this, Johnny thought, grabbing the volleyball from his knapsack.

"Uh, remember I told you guys about Kylie Smith?"

"The babe from Spring Valley who's working here?" Danny asked. "Didn't the entire freshman class—the guys, I mean—go to every swim meet last year just to see her in a bathing suit?"

Kevin nodded and let out a whistle. "She's the one your girlfriend's hated since like fourth grade or something."

Johnny smiled. "Guess who my new partner is. And guess who's also going to Allman."

28

"Oh, man," Kevin said gleefully, "the fates really fried your butt this time."

The three Ford brothers got into position and tossed a volleyball back and forth, warming up. "You're dog meat," Danny said, stretching his arms behind his back. "Worse, mutt meat."

Three beach dudes out for a run jogged over and challenged them to a game. Johnny nodded. They could use practice against live prey to tune up for the tournament—a mere eight days away. The guys introduced themselves, and they positioned themselves on the other side of the net.

"Ready when you are, dude," the big one said.

Johnny turned to his brothers, ball against his chest. "If I wanted commentary like that, I would've gone on *Ricki Lake*. What I need is advice. What do I tell Jane? It's bad enough that Kylie and I are working together. But going to the same school? That's an extinction-level event." Johnny batted the ball to Kevin.

Kevin pumped the ball to Danny. "Absolutely do not tell her, Johnny. Anything. At all. You shouldn't even have told her you and Kylie are in the same town together. Don't blow it by telling her you're sharing a chair." He wiped sweat from his face. "And you were sitting awfully close to her in that chair, dude."

Johnny scowled and smacked the ball away. "What chair were you looking at? We were just doing our jobs."

Danny shrugged and smiled. "Just telling you

29

what I could see from the poolside, Johnny. The eyes don't lie."

"You're full of it," Johnny shot back. "You can hardly even see the beach from the pool."

"Dudes . . . ," came the voice of one of the guys across the net.

Kevin held up a hand to the dudes and tipped the ball back to Danny. "Maybe this whole thing is a test to see if you and Jane are meant for each other. Fate couldn't send a better candidate than a hot blonde who happens to be Jane's enemy, right?"

"You and fate," Johnny grumbled, shaking his head.

Kevin laughed. "Hey, big bro, I'm just trying to smooth your trip into oblivion, that's all. Your butt's fried, and you need all the help you can get."

"Don't remind me," Johnny replied grimly.

"Dudes . . ."

Danny held the ball against his chest as he turned to Johnny. "There's definitely only one way out of this. If you tell Jane, you're bound to get the ultimatum: Quit your job, transfer to a new school, or else. On the other hand, Jane still hates this girl, so not telling her would be just as bad. But by not telling her, it would take a tactical mistake for her to find out. If you're smart, that won't happen. Which means your only course of action is to definitely not tell her. The less she knows, the happier she shall be."

Johnny shook his head.

"Dudes," came the now irritated voice of one of the beach dudes across the net.

The Fords turned.

"Serve already!" the big guy said, arms spread in anticipation. "Serve!"

The brothers declared themselves ready, taking up their normal positions around the court. Johnny tried to put Kylie out of his mind—no easy feat—and concentrate on the game. He had to. Their moment of truth—the tournament—was coming quickly, and the whole summer was going to boil down to that moment. Johnny refused to screw it up.

The beach dudes weren't very good volleyball players. The Fords quickly took a five-to-one lead. The three strangers were definitely game, though. For every point they lost, one of them uttered some kind of declaration/curse/mantra that always began with the word *dude*.

When Johnny spiked the Fords' sixth point: "Dude . . . ousted!"

Point eight: "Dude . . . denied!"

Ten: "Dude . . . embalmed!"

When the dudes won their second hopeful point: "Dude . . . retort!"

The fast volleys allowed Johnny and his brothers to get into a tight rhythm. The stress of the day evaporated as Johnny felt only the sand under his feet. The sting of the ball. The clean drops of sweat rolling down his brow and back. This was what he envisioned during the tournament: the Fords working in perfect sync, the logical reward for literally years of practice and playing together. Danny's serves, Kevin's sets, Johnny's spikes.

They worked like a machine. Like a charm. Pick your simile; the Fords were *on*.

Point twenty-one: "Dude . . . *dead*."

The Fords high-fived and then shook hands with the beach dudes, who were obviously shocked at the creaming they took. But they were mellow enough not to get upset. They wished the Fords *"bonne chance,* dudes," and walked off into the sunrise.

Johnny was satisfied with their play. "If we hit like that next Saturday, we should be okay."

"My serve was working overtime," Danny said, strutting. "I got game."

"What you got is BO, butt head," Kevin muttered, tossing the ball at him.

Their words faded out of Johnny's ears. On the final point his mind immediately went back to Kylie. He wasn't sure about the plan not to tell Jane. That was the same as lying, after all. And Johnny really didn't think he could keep Kylie's presence a secret. Jane would no doubt visit him on the beach while they worked. And Kylie would no doubt go to the volleyball tournament, where Jane would be.

If two locomotives leave Spring Valley High School at the same time, traveling at different speeds, when would they collide?

Pretty soon, it seemed.

"You desperately need a distraction," Kevin remarked, shaking his head.

Danny shoved Kevin aside, Three Stooges style. "You're all tied up in knots for nothing. You've done nothing wrong here, pal. You're a victim of circumstance. If Jane is too much of a meanie to understand that, I say tough tuna."

"That's brilliant," Johnny replied, sighing.

"Don't take this the wrong way, Johnny," Kevin offered. "No offense meant. But seriously, what's with Jane? Why do you like her so much?"

Johnny glared at his brother. "Say what?"

Kevin held up his hands. "Don't get me wrong. She's pretty and all. But she's kind of a stick-in-the-mud."

"More like a foot in the grave," Danny added.

Johnny balled his fists but kept his cool. "You guys are way out of line."

Kevin shook his head. "No, Johnny, we aren't. Because in the past two months you've passed judgment on our girlfriends without really knowing them at all. Well, we *know* Jane. We've known her for three years. And she's about to turn the rest of your summer into quicksand, and you didn't even do anything wrong. All we want to know is, what's her problem?"

"I know what her problem is," Danny declared. "To me, the mystery is why you're still with her."

Johnny scowled. He couldn't believe this. With everything that was going on, he needed brotherly judgment like he needed a punch in the head. "You guys don't know her. We love each other. It's that simple."

"Because you're the same person," Kevin offered, spinning the volleyball on a finger. "That's why you get along so well."

Johnny knew that was true. But didn't that

mean they were meant for each other? Opposites were supposed to attract, but like-minded people could get along pretty well too. He and Jane had been together since the summer after ninth grade. They were both serious people. They had goals. He and Jane had avoided the goofball nonsense that seemed to run the lives of everyone else they knew. Maybe that was why they were named Class Couple—because they seemed so right together. And not because of longevity, which Kylie had been talking about.

But just because he and Jane were so alike that they didn't always have a good time didn't mean Jane wasn't a great person. Life wasn't about fun all the time. It was about working hard to achieve your goals.

Don't tell her, he ordered himself. *It's not worth the aggravation this close to the tournament. Danny's right. I've done nothing wrong. It wasn't my fault Beach assigned Kylie to my chair. And we've had enough distractions from v-ball. We don't need another. Not this close to the opening serve . . .*

But as the brothers made their way back to the apartment for quick showers before work, Johnny had a gnawing in his gut that wouldn't go away. It was the uncomfortable feeling that he was now a liar.

Three

"JOHNNY, C'MON," DANNY said a half hour later, slinging his knapsack over his shoulder. "We're gonna be late."

"Whoa," Kevin added, downing a gulp of orange juice (from the carton, of course). "This is a first. Us dragging Johnny out the door to work! Man, he is in serious trouble."

But Johnny wasn't going anywhere. Not yet. Not until—

"Guys, go without me." Johnny sat on the recliner and opened his knapsack, pretending to be rooting around for something. "There's something I need to do."

"What?" Kevin asked.

"Mind your own business," Johnny muttered, gesturing at them to shoo. "Guys, get going. You're gonna be late."

Kevin and Danny looked at Johnny, then at each other. Kevin shrugged.

"Oh, so tell us your business, and then tell us to butt out," Danny complained.

"Beat it," Johnny told them. "I'll catch up with you."

When they closed the door behind them, Johnny took a deep breath, then reached for the phone.

It took six minutes for Jane to make it from the huge cafeteria where she'd been eating breakfast with her group down the hill to the camp office. "Johnny?"

"Hey," he said, feeling the dread like a rock in his stomach.

"What's wrong?" she asked nervously.

"Um, nothing," he told her. "I, um, just wanted to talk to you. How's camp?"

"Johnny, it's a quarter to nine in the morning. If you're calling this early, there has to be a reason. A bad reason. Did something happen to Kevin or Danny? Oh my God, is one of them in the hospital?"

"No, no," Johnny said. "Nothing like that. Really, I just wanted to say hi and, um, finish our convo from last night. You had to go. Remember?"

Jane laughed. "The cookie fight."

"Right," Johnny said. "So, did you resolve it?"

"The cookie fight?" Jane asked incredulously. "Johnny, are you okay?"

Stop stalling, he told himself. *She knows something's up. She hears it in your voice. She's concerned. She doesn't suspect anything weird; she's just reacting to your mood. Because she cares.*

Tell her.

Suddenly the front door burst open, and Kevin bounded in. "Forgot my—" He trailed off, narrowing

36

his eyes at Johnny. Kevin eyed the cordless, then Johnny's tense expression. "Don't even think about it," Kevin mouthed as he grabbed his wallet from between the sofa cushions. "You'll so regret it."

Johnny glanced at Kevin and shrugged. Kevin rolled his eyes and was gone again.

Tell her.

Johnny's mind spun. Not telling her would keep the peace—maybe. But deep down, where the real decisions got made, Johnny knew that not telling Jane about Kylie was the exact same thing as lying to her. And he'd never lied to Jane before. Ever.

Tell her.

Before he knew it, he was speaking in a strangely cheerful voice. "Um, last night I was about to tell you something before you had to go."

"Tell me what?" She sounded nervous.

"Um, just about my day." He cleared his throat. "A surfer almost ran over an old lady with her board. And I was assigned a new lifeguard partner. It's sort of funny, in a way."

"Why?" Jane asked.

Johnny heard his throat click as he swallowed. "Well . . . you'll never guess who my partner is."

"Who?"

Johnny chuckled nervously. "Guess."

"Johnny, you just said I'll never guess."

"Oh, okay. It's Kylie Smith."

Johnny was met with absolute dead silence.

When Jane finally answered, her voice was ice-cold. "Are you kidding?"

Johnny tried to remain upbeat, like, hey, this was no big deal. "Nope. My boss made it official this morning."

"I can't believe this," Jane muttered.

"Me either," Johnny replied. "I mean, I knew she was working down here for the summer, but there are something like seventy lifeguard stations in Surf City. What are the odds?"

"Exactly," Jane said flatly.

"What do you mean?"

"I mean this was probably her idea," Jane replied. "She probably *requested* the transfer. She probably tried to get partnered with you all summer and finally got her way."

"Huh?" Johnny had no idea what Jane was talking about. "Why would she want to work with me? I've never said five words to the girl in my life."

"Exactly again." Jane let out a low whistle. "She clearly never got to you in high school, so she's making her final attempt now."

Johnny racked his brain for a second to try to figure out what she meant. "Jane, what are you talking about?"

"Johnny! Duh! She hates my guts. So she's going after my boyfriend."

He blinked. *Say what?*

"No way, Jane." Johnny shook his head. "First of all, lifeguards can only ask for a transfer. They can't request a *specific* gig. And second, Beach puts people where he wants them no matter what anyone thinks. He's a real hard hat that way."

"This is just like Kylie," Jane snapped. "She'd do it just to get to me."

"I don't buy it," Johnny said. "She doesn't seem like the type to—"

"Oh, really?" Jane challenged. "How do you know? Do you think you know her after one day? Are you two best friends now?"

Johnny sighed. He knew this would happen. Great. Now his own brothers could told-you-so him all day. Maybe he *should* start taking advice from fifteen-year-olds. If he'd listened to Kev and Danny, he wouldn't be having this conversation. And he wouldn't be late to work.

"Look, Jane," Johnny said. "I know this really bothers you, but you can't worry about it. You know me. It's just a job. She's just my partner. It's no big deal. I'll be civil to her, of course—I mean, I've gotta be. But don't get upset about that. Please? I think she's way over whatever went on between you two anyway. She all but said so."

"Oh, so you two were talking about me?" Johnny felt Jane's mood shift even harder, edging into rage country. "What exactly did she say about me?"

You're just digging yourself in deeper and deeper, Johnny told himself. He didn't want the conversation to go in this direction, but he'd stepped right into it. Now if he wasn't careful, the whole thing could blow up in his face.

"She didn't really say anything," Johnny replied calmly. "I asked her what happened in the seventh grade. She told me the same thing you told me.

39

Except she also said that she didn't hate you at all. She was vague about the fight and didn't want to talk about it. I left it at that. And that's all. The rest was about life guarding."

Johnny inwardly cringed, knowing he was leaving out quite a bit, including the fact that he and Kylie were both headed for Allman College. Johnny knew that little tidbit would send Jane over the edge. Now wasn't the time to tell her.

She's going to find out sooner or later, he thought. He preferred later. Much later.

"This is unbelievable," Jane moaned. "Just unbelievable."

Johnny took a deep breath. "Jane, I know this really stinks from your end. But it's not that bad. Kylie's a pro. We're lifeguard partners, and that's it. There really isn't that much to talk about."

"There's everything to talk about, Johnny," Jane countered. "You don't know what it's like. You don't know what *she's* like. She's going after you to spite me. One big, final slap in the face. Trust me—she'll be shyly flirting with you at work today. Tomorrow she'll share some sob story to make you feel bad for her. The next day she'll invite you for a walk on the boardwalk just to talk it over. The next day, *bam*. She's kissing you."

Johnny had never seen—heard—this side of Jane. On the one hand, she was justifiably upset. Her enemy, rival, whatever, was sitting next to her boyfriend every day—in a bathing suit. But then again, Jane and Kylie were still "enemies" over something that had happened a long, long time ago. Something that probably meant absolutely nothing to either of them.

And besides, wasn't he allowed to form his own opinion of Kylie?

"Jane, you know me, right? If I even *sense* she's up to something like you said, I'll be on guard. Don't worry, sweetie, okay?"

Jane sighed. "You don't know what she's capable of, Johnny. You've never seen her in action. You *don't* know her."

Johnny considered that. Jane was the most level-headed person he knew. Was it possible that she was right? *Was* he just a pawn in some immature revenge plot against Jane? He *had* only spent one day with Kylie. A working day. Jane was right: He *didn't* know her.

"Jane, listen to me," Johnny said. "You'll be here in a week. After that, it's just you and me. Kylie is not a part of this equation. You won't even have to see her."

"Fine," Jane replied angrily.

"Jeez, Jane, what do you expect me to do? Quit my job?"

Silence.

"Jane!"

"Just don't forget what's between us, Johnny," she told him. "That's what I want."

"How could I forget?" Johnny replied. "I love you, Jane. You know that."

"I was talking about what's between Kylie and me," Jane replied coldly.

A twinge of anger hit Johnny. Jane couldn't forget about Kylie long enough to listen to what he'd just said? This whole thing was quickly getting ridiculous. This went back to the seventh grade, for crying out loud! Who remembered what they did in the seventh grade? Who cared? The three of them had graduated!

"I'm trying to see this from your point of view, Jane," he said. "But I need you to be reasonable. You'll be here soon, and you'll see this isn't some major intergalactic life-guarding conspiracy dreamed up by a pathological girl on a seventh-grade power trip. Kylie's just a lifeguard, and she's just my partner. That's it, end of story."

Jane paused, then let out a long, frustrated sigh. "No, Johnny. I don't think it is. I think this story's just beginning."

Johnny arrived at the Surf City Resort Hotel's employee entrance only ten minutes late. Not bad. What *was* bad was the fact that Jane's words had echoed in his head during the entire bike ride like some sick chorus to a song that ran on a never-ending tape loop in his skull: *Remember what's between us.*

Like he said, how could he forget?

Johnny thought back to what he was like in the seventh grade. Mostly he was confused. Everything was in flux in the seventh grade: his mind, his body, his personality, even his voice, for crying out loud. Insecurity was like a giant zit: Everyone had it; everyone tried to cover it up as best they could. But the insecurity always reared its cretin head at the worst times. The result was usually embarrassment of epic proportions. Johnny supposed if the humiliation was severe enough, it could indeed sting years later.

He thought back to his own dealings with embarrassment. Wendy Capriotti, his girlfriend of four hours, had told their entire seventh-grade class that he was a terrible kisser. Johnny had been mortified. Luckily, though, he'd been one smooth dude even then. He'd told the girls Wendy was lying—because *he'd* dumped *her* for being the bad kisser. That was true. And he'd added that any girl could kiss him if she wanted to find out who was lying.

Johnny had kissed more girls in seventh grade than eighth and ninth combined. He'd been vindicated. And Wendy had been humiliated in return. No guy would go near her after that; well, for the next day anyway, because they all figured she was a horrible kisser. Luckily for Wendy, she'd filled out very nicely one year later and had her pick of idiots. She'd even forgiven Johnny and made out with him again. Her kissing hadn't improved, though.

That was seventh-grade-type nonsense. He'd beat Wendy at her own game, but he got her back good. Who could imagine Wendy holding a grudge against him for five years for that silliness?

Cheerleading and a guy. *Please*. Like it was any more serious than Johnny's "big feud" with Wendy.

Johnny locked up his bike, collected his gear,

and ran down to the chair. It wasn't Kylie he was rushing to. After that conversation with Jane, he was anything but revved up for a day of work next to a potential shark. Not that he believed Kylie was a shark. He just wasn't ruling it out. From what he'd seen of the girl, she was okay.

He rushed down because he was late. Johnny Ford, reporting late for duty for the first time in his life. He noticed Kylie wasn't up in the chair. Scanning the beach, he spotted her knee-deep in the water, separating two young boys who were fighting.

"Pull your hair," she said to the redhead.

"Huh?" the kid replied.

"C'mon, give it a good, hard tug." The redhead did as she said and let out a yelp. "See? Hurts, huh? Now you know how he feels when you pull his hair."

"Yeah, but he hit me!" the redhead argued.

Kylie turned to the blond kid. "Give yourself a whack on the arm. Go ahead." The blond glared at the redhead, then punched himself on the bicep. He let out a yelp too. "Okay, so now you know how it feels to be hit."

Johnny realized he was smiling. He changed his expression to neutral and pretended to be casually observing.

"Here's the deal, guys: hair pulling and hitting aren't allowed on the beach. Or anywhere. Didn't you two know that?"

The boys exchanged glances. "So I guess he can't pull my hair anymore," the blond said.

"Yeah, and he can't hit me ever again," the red-head added.

Kylie smiled. "Exactly. So, since you can't do any of that stuff anymore, what are you gonna do instead?"

The two kids traded glances. "Swim?" the blond asked.

"Right!" Kylie announced. "Excellent!"

"Or, um, play video games at the arcade on the boardwalk?" the redhead threw in, clearly not willing to miss being praised.

"Exactly! Perfect!" Kylie told them with a big smile. "I have a great idea. Why don't you guys have fun swimming for a while, then go play some video games and then maybe even have some hot dogs?"

"Race ya!" the redhead yelled, and went charging into the Pacific. The blond took off after him.

Kylie headed to the chair. She stopped short when she noticed Johnny standing, arms crossed in front of it, slowly shaking his head. "You're amazing. I've never seen anyone handle kids or a situation like that the way you did in my life! You were really just incredible!"

Kylie beamed and joined Johnny by the chair. They both looked out at the water for a moment. The little terrors were splashing each other and doing their own version of cannonballs. Kylie laughed. "Kids don't want to fight. And they don't want to be yelled at over it either. They want someone to take the pressure away, that's all. Once that's done, they're back playing again, totally forgetting they hated each other a second ago."

45

"I hope you're planning a career with kids," Johnny said as he climbed up to the chair. Kylie followed. "Not enough people have your mind-set, patience, or creativity when it comes to solving problems with tykes."

Kylie grinned and bit her lower lip. "I'm planning to major in psychology—but who knows, maybe I'll end up focusing on child psychology. I do love kids."

Johnny couldn't help comparing the way Kylie had handled her kid fiasco to the way Jane had dealt with the cookie-monster fight. Jane had yelled and punished them by not allowing snacks that night or dessert the next day.

Stop it, he told himself. *How dare you compare the two of them? So what if Jane isn't good at settling kid wars?*

Feeling like a traitor, he settled back against the cushion.

"Sure is a hot one, huh?" she asked, rubbing sunblock on her nose.

Any girl who was trying to steal her rival's boyfriend wouldn't make her nose stark white while sitting right next to him. Jane had to be wrong.

"Yeah," he agreed, rubbing his own lotion on his arms. "It's gonna be a scorcher." The sun was extra hot this morning, a pure southern California bake off that began at nine in the morning and wouldn't let up until sunset. A fine sheen of sweat was already coating both of them. Kylie wiped her face with a towel.

If Jane had seen how Kylie had handled the fighting kids, surely she'd agree that Kylie was a good, warm person. Actually, he thought, Jane would probably think that Kylie had sugarcoated their behavior and let them off without discipline. Right and wrong. Black and white. Serious.

But—

But whatever.

"So, just out of curiosity," Kylie began, her eyes trained on the water, "did you tell Jane we're partners?"

He glanced at her. Her expression was serious, not sarcastic or even remotely devilish. "Yup. I told her this morning. That's why I was late."

She laughed. "So I take it she didn't jump for joy."

Johnny tightened his lips and shook his head.

"Figures you told her," Kylie said. "You could have gotten away with not mentioning it. I would have made myself scarce while she was here." She leaned forward and scanned the water, twirling her whistle on one finger. "The poor girl's probably tied in knots right now."

Johnny sighed, picturing Jane's workday at camp: bows and arrows and little Hiawathas. "Not telling her would be equal to lying."

Kylie nodded. "I always heard that about you at school, that you were aboveboard. And around the beach, of course. Some say you're Mr. Rules."

Johnny's cheeks grew hot. People talked about him? What was so terrible about not being a goof-off slacker?

"You're honest," Kylie continued. "But I wonder about something. I wonder if it's wrong to lie when omitting something would save the other person's feelings. Yeah, you didn't lie to Jane. But now she feels horrible. So which is really better? Keeping the truth from someone or hurting them by telling them?"

"All I know," Johnny said, "is that if I hadn't told her and she found out, she'd be furious at me. Not because of you, but because I didn't *tell* her. So telling her was the right thing to do."

Kylie tilted her head at him. "I guess that's a good point. I don't know, Johnny. I'm not too sure which I think is right."

"You're an interesting girl, Kylie Smith," he said, stretching out his legs. "Here you are again, sympathizing with the feelings of a girl you don't even like. Most people would think you'd be happy she was upset."

Kylie shook her head. "Now, *that* is seventh grade. Anyway, she has a right to be upset. If my boyfriend was four hours away working with a girl who thought he was totally great, I'd be upset too."

Totally great? Johnny suddenly found himself sitting up straighter, his chest puffed out a bit. Okay, so the compliment had affected him. Being referred to as totally great by someone he was coming to think of as totally great was . . . totally great.

Hey, wait a minute, he thought. Was she making her interest known? Had Jane been right about Kylie after all? Was Kylie going after Jane's boyfriend for revenge?

Jeez—revenge for what? This was silly. He wasn't

even going to think about this for one second more.

"Why don't we change the subject?" Johnny offered.

"Good idea," she said, blowing her whistle at a kid who'd swum beyond the red-flag boundaries.

"So how'd you end up here as my partner anyway? Did you request a transfer because you didn't like your old partner?"

"More like he didn't like me—anymore," Kylie explained, her eyes downcast. "We were dating—until I found out I was sharing him."

Johnny glanced at her. "Sorry. I didn't mean to get personal."

"I think we're beyond that point, don't you?" she said, offering him a weak smile. "I knew Paul was kind of egotistical, but he was smart and funny and took his job really seriously. I guess I fell for his lines—or wanted to believe them. The other girl didn't even care that he'd been two timing her with me. She's still seeing him. She's a Fizz Cola girl. You know, the ones who walk around the beaches in teeny-weeny bikinis, handing out Fizz freebies?"

"Uh-oh," Johnny said.

"Yep. She worked my beach. Which meant that after I caught Paul making out with her on the boardwalk and broke up with him—very dramatically, of course—they would come to the beach every day, hanging all over each other. It was like he wanted to show me that I didn't matter. That I never mattered."

Johnny reached over and squeezed her hand. "I'm sorry you got hurt."

Today she'll tell you some sob story, tomorrow you'll be walking on the boardwalk, next day you'll be kissing her. . . .

Johnny froze for a second. No way was Kylie making this up. He sneaked a peek at her; she definitely looked somber. She was staring out at the water, twirling her whistle, her expression saddened.

"I was so happy when Beach paired us, Johnny," she said, turning to face him. "I was thrilled, actually. It was as if the fates had heard my prayers."

Johnny coughed. Oh. My. God. The fates? She was all but admitting she was going after him! Was she about to say: *and sent me here to steal you away from that beach-hating, unfun, grudge-holder Jane . . .*

"Why?" he barely managed to croak out, shifting a bit away from her.

"Because I knew that of all the lifeguards at Surf City," she began, "you'd *never* hit on me. Not Johnny Ford, boyfriend extraordinaire. After my disaster with Paul, the last thing I need is to fall for another guy. I'm taking a much needed break."

Huh. So much for the man-eating ogre.

Suddenly he was struck with the notion that Jane had really missed out. She and Kylie had been friends, and their stupid fight had ended things. But she'd missed out on a warm, compassionate, sweet person in her life, someone who Jane would have really admired.

It wasn't his fault that he'd gotten to know a girl he'd never had the opportunity to talk to. He'd assumed she was the evil queen Jane had made her

50

out to be. But as for Jane's continued war with her, Johnny was pretty much convinced that this was a one-sided war. To Jane, the battle still raged. But to Kylie, the conflict had faded away a long time ago.

He wondered how Paul could have cheated on Kylie, even with a Fizz Cola girl. Kylie was a babe. And a smart, funny, fun babe. Fizz girl was just that: fizz. Which went flat pretty quickly.

If I were Kylie's boyfriend, I'd never look at another girl—

Johnny's eyes widened at the thought that had just run through his brain.

The smell of cocoa butter drifted over, and he shifted back over a bit. Closer.

Man, that smelled good. He peeked over at the glistening lotion on Kylie's tanned legs.

Suddenly Jane's face floated into mind. Beautiful Jane, his girlfriend of three years. Her almond-shaped brown eyes with gold flecks. Her long, brown hair. Her long legs. Jane, who was four hours away, very upset at the moment because of him. And what was Johnny, her devoted boyfriend extra-ordinaire doing? Moving closer to the girl she hated.

Not cool.

Johnny looked at his watch. As of right now, he was adopting a professional working relationship with Kylie. He'd be polite and friendly, but that was it. No talking about Jane behind her back. No talking about cheating boyfriends. No talking about how totally great he was.

Because Johnny had almost become totally interested . . .

Four

THREE RAPID-FIRE DAYS passed.

In that time Johnny had actually settled into a routine with Kylie. They worked so well together that he almost wished she'd been his partner all summer. They got along fine, and the beach ran smoothly.

Outwardly, that is.

Johnny had a system: He barely looked at Kylie. If he didn't look at her, he wouldn't stare at her. Which he wanted to do. When she spoke to him, he kept his eyes on the water, just like he was supposed to. That way he could kid himself into believing that he wasn't attracted to her.

So far, it worked just fine.

Jane had called every night. She always asked about Kylie, sometimes before she asked about him—which ticked Johnny off to no end. He finally called her on it, which started an argument that ended in Jane hanging up. And calling back three minutes later to apologize.

It was a roller coaster. But strangely enough, between Jane and the intense practice sessions he and his brothers were having, the only calm Johnny got was at work, when responsible, hardworking Kylie was sitting, twirling her whistle, cool in her shades and in her whole outlook.

Not that Johnny didn't find the situation with Kylie draining. He'd trained his brain to react to logic, to facts and figures. He was geared to make money, which required strong decision making and specific goals. But this? This was the female mind, something Johnny didn't understand. He didn't understand why Jane had to hang on to this ancient grudge. He didn't understand what drove her anger. And he certainly didn't understand why she still felt threatened.

But then there was the stuff he did understand. Like how Jane felt being stranded four hours away while her boyfriend spent his days becoming better and better friends with a girl she despised. Or how Kylie was growing on him . . . in a very powerful way. Powerful enough for him to be consciously aware of her beautiful presence every minute of the day. Powerful enough for Johnny to actually *want* to go to work.

Just go about your business, pal, he told himself. *You vowed to keep your distance three days ago, and you're doing fine.*

Monday dawned like every day in southern

California: the luminous sunshine polishing everything to a hot, silver sheen. The sand reached foot-warming temperature by ten. The surf was alive, with waves pounding and whitecaps whipping out on the water. A riptide warning had been issued, but so far there had been no problems broadcast on their radios. Johnny and Kylie simply planted their swimming flags a little closer to the chair and watched the wealthy hotel guests splash their way to happiness.

"You're quiet this afternoon," Kylie probed, nudging him. "Not that you haven't been the past few days."

He stole a peek at her, then focused on the water. "Just thinking about the tournament."

"Ah," she said, "I thought maybe you were having problems being partnered with me."

Johnny twirled his whistle. What was he supposed to say to that? And why was Kylie so direct? Didn't she know you were supposed to hem and haw and mince words and beat around the bush so long, you just forgot the point? If a good thing did come out of sharing the chair with Kylie, maybe it would be learning how to say what was on his mind without worrying so much.

"It's just that my brothers and I have been practicing every morning before work," Johnny explained, completely ignoring her comment, "and we haven't played so hot the past few days."

"Isn't it supposed to be a good idea to take a breather a few days before the event?" Kylie asked.

"Give your body time to rest for the big game?"

"Probably," he said. "We're just so worried. We could sure use that money."

"Well, well, well. Buick or Chevrolet or whatever your dumb car name is has a new lifeguard partner. And isn't she a sweetums!"

Johnny groaned. Tanner St. John was strolling up the beach, kicking sand. Like twin engines on either side of him were Shooter Ridge and Arliss Neeson, Tanner's partners in volleyball crime. The trio was the team to beat in the upcoming tournament. And Tanner liked to remind everyone of that fact at all times.

The trio were too tall and too built up and had too much hair. Tanner actually wore his in a ponytail. Johnny had always thought only stoners could get away with that without looking cheesy.

"You can forget about taking home that prize money, Pontiac," Tanner said. "You are gonna lose. You're gonna make a total fool of yourself in front of everyone."

"Yeah, him and those two geek brothers of his," Shooter Ridge announced, his thick arms folded across his chest. "Oh, wait. The three of them won't even make it to the court. 'Ooh, the sand is too hot, the sand is too hot!' " He danced on the sand for emphasis.

The trio broke into snorting gales of laughter. Tanner turned his attention to Kylie. "Hey, sugar. Did the hotel put you out here as eye candy to lure us to the beach?"

Kylie sat straight up. "You're an idiot."

Tanner smirked. "Ouch. That hurt. Say, Ford, what is it with your family and their smart-mouthed chicks? You gonna send the team of chickies to play v-ball for you?"

Johnny just smiled. "This is a private beach, jerk. Which means you have exactly one minute to do an about-face and walk your Speedo-wearing butt off this stretch."

Tanner's perfectly capped grin stretched wide. He exchanged amused looks with Shooter and Arliss. "Oh, I'm dying to see this. Just dying to see you and Buffy kick us off this beach."

Johnny returned the grin. "Actually, we can't do that. We're on duty and have a responsibility to the people in the water. So what we do in situations like this is pick up our little radios here"—he held up a walkie-talkie for emphasis—"and call security. You've seen the hotel's security force, right, Tan? I'd run if I were you."

Kylie snickered.

Tanner scowled. "Come down off that chair."

"Tanner, get lost, okay? We've got a job to do here, and you're distracting us."

"Oh yeah, like you loser lifeguards do anything but sit on those stupid chairs with your stupid white noses and whistles and check out the scene."

Suddenly a scream came from the surf. Johnny shot up, grabbed the Excalibur, and jumped down, shading his eyes to check out what was happening as he ran to the water. A figure flailed its arms about thirty yards out. Another figure next to it was a lump in the water, motionless.

"Call it in," Johnny shouted behind his shoulder to Kylie.

Johnny dove headfirst into the cold smack of a wave, letting Excalibur trail behind him. He furiously pumped his arms and legs in a powerful freestyle toward the men.

Fifteen yards, he measured. *A few more seconds.*

He could now see that the flailing swimmer—a middle-aged man—wasn't the one in trouble. The man was trying to keep the motionless person next to him afloat. He wasn't having much success.

On his next breath Johnny glanced behind him. Kylie stood onshore, waving a red flag high in the air to alert the paramedics to their exact location on the beach. A crowd was gathering on the beach.

Adrenaline drove him forward. Johnny had helped cramped swimmers out of the water, but he'd never had to do a serious rescue before. He'd never had to rescue an unconscious person.

Don't think, he warned himself. *Just let training and instinct take over.*

But was he trained enough? Did he know enough? Could he really help someone?

Don't think!

He reached the pair seconds later. The middle-aged man was panicked. His eyes were wide, his face pale. The unconscious man was faceup in the water. Johnny immediately slid between them, roping his arms around the unconscious man's torso and propping him up. His head rolled limply to the side.

"I don't think he's breathing!" his friend shouted. "His name's Harold O'Hearn. He's vacationing here."

Johnny floated the unconscious Harold O'Hearn on his back and half swam, half dragged the inert body to shore. A sick feeling came over him: He could feel no life in the man.

Don't die on me! Don't you dare!

Johnny kicked and pulled against the tide, careful to keep the old man's face above water. A massive crowd had formed on the beach now. Women with hands over their mouths. Men gaping. Children wide-eyed.

Johnny's toes clawed sand. Kylie and the two lifeguards who worked the stretch on either side ran in knee-deep to help carry Harold out and lay him down on the sand. Johnny immediately began sweeping the man's mouth with his fingers.

"Is he breathing?" Kylie asked.

"No!" Johnny shouted. "I'm gonna perform CPR."

Kylie knelt on the other side of Harold. "Help's on the way." She pinched the man's wrist and placed two fingers on his throat. Johnny caught a subtle widening of her eyes. He felt the same surge of barely controlled panic before she even uttered the words, "No pulse."

"Let's do it! Now!" Johnny said.

He did chest compressions while Kylie did mouth-to-mouth. He was dimly aware of the sound of sirens getting closer. Dimly aware of hushed voices. If fear had a sound, Johnny now knew what it was.

"Come on, Harold O'Hearn," Johnny ordered, pressing in conjunction with Kylie's timed breaths. "You're a fighter, man! Fight! Breathe! Come on, Harold. You can do it! Breathe! Breathe!"

The old man's body convulsed beneath him, and there was a gurgling cough. The man spit water out of his mouth, then coughed more. He sat up, clearly disoriented. But he was breathing.

Johnny froze, paralyzed. Kylie closed her eyes as if offering silent thanks to the fates, then fell back on her elbows, catching her own breath. "Are you okay, Kylie?" he asked.

She could only nod.

"What—," Harold barely managed to squeak out.

The paramedics raced down the beach. Johnny put a hand on his shoulder. "I think you caught a nasty wave out there, Mr. O'Hearn. The paramedics are here, and they're going to take you to Surf City General to make sure you're A-OK for swimming tomorrow."

The old man nodded and gave Johnny and Kylie a weak smile.

"He's okay!" someone in the crowd finally declared. "They did it. He's alive!"

"Harold!" his friend shouted, rushing toward him. "You had us all worried sick!"

Applause erupted all around them.

Johnny and Kylie let out a breath in unison, then fell back on the sand. He turned his head to her; she did the same. He noticed she had one hand over her heart, the way he did. His was racing a mile a minute.

She reached over and laid her hand on top of his.

He wondered if she could feel his heart racing two miles a minute now. . . .

"Dude. Unbelievable. Wild. Way to go."

Danny and Kevin clapped Johnny on the shoulder. Johnny nodded his thanks, still feeling the lingering twitch of adrenaline in his system. The circus had pretty much run its course. Four other lifeguards had responded to the backup call, including Beach McGriff, who'd praised Johnny and Kylie for how they handled the rescue. Even the owner of the hotel, Kevin's own girlfriend's father, had rushed out of his tower office to personally make sure the guests were calm—then he'd made a fuss over Johnny and Kylie. There was also a smattering of police and a full-blown EMT crew with ambulance. Harold O'Hearn was able to talk in full sentences by the time the EMTs loaded him into the ambulance.

"What do I need a hospital for?" Harold demanded. "I feel fine!"

"Sir—"

Harold's eyes bugged. "Don't you 'sir' me!" He struggled to sit up on the gurney. "We're not going anywhere until I talk to the two who pulled me out. Where are those kids?"

"He's definitely okay," Harold's friend said with a smile. "Back to his old self already!"

Johnny and Kylie were ushered to the ambulance. Johnny had to admit the guy looked pretty good for having been clinically dead less than a half hour earlier. His cheeks were ruddy, and the fire was definitely in his eyes. His gray hair flared out in all directions except for the bald spot on his head. When he saw Johnny and Kylie, his expression softened.

"C'mere, you two," he ordered, waving them forward. Then he vigorously shook each of their hands. "I want you to know how grateful I am. What're your names?"

"I'm Johnny," Johnny said.

"Kylie."

"Okay, Johnny and Kylie," Harold said. "You saved my butt today. I won't forget that. You ask anyone at this crummy hotel, and they'll tell you Harold O'Hearn knows how to take care of those who take care of him. Understand?"

"We were just doing our jobs, Mr. O'Hearn," Kylie replied.

His grin widened. "Listen to her, will you? Well, get this, Kylie: You did one heck of a job today. And I want you both to know that if there is anything—anything at all—that I can do for you, just let me know. I mean that. You hear?"

Johnny nodded. "Thanks, Mr. O'Hearn."

"It's the least I can do," Mr. O'Hearn said.

"Okay, fellas, time to go." The EMTs lifted the gurney into the back of the ambulance. Before they slammed the doors on him, Harold sat up and called out, "By the way, Kylie, that was the best kiss I've had in twenty-seven years!"

Everyone laughed. Kylie's cheeks reddened. And the ambulance pulled away across the sand. As the crowd dissipated, the other lifeguards came over to pay their respects in handshakes and high fives. Beach flashed his surfer grin.

"That your first dead in the water?" Beach asked them.

Johnny and Kylie both nodded.

"Congrats, kids," Beach said. "You're real lifeguards now. You can be real proud of the work you did here today. You saved a man's life."

"A rich man's life," Kevin Ford added, smirking.

Danny's ears perked up. "How rich?"

"Thirty years in Silicon Valley real estate," Kevin replied. "He tried to buy the 49ers a few years ago, but his partners crapped out on the Pacific Exchange. But rumor has it he's worth a quarter-bil plus."

Johnny shook his head. "You've been listening to poolside gossip for too long, little brother."

Beach stepped forward, interrupting. "Well, dudes and dudettes, I've got sand to prowl. And I would be totally remiss if I didn't give our two saviors here the rest of the afternoon off."

"Off?" Johnny asked. "Really?"

Beach nodded. "You really think you'd be any good on this beach after what just happened? Go home and get some rest. I'll cover for you."

"Thanks, Beach," Johnny said.

"Nope, dude," Beach replied, giving Johnny a wink. "Thank *you*."

Five

AFTER EVERYONE LEFT, Johnny quickly noticed that Kylie had disappeared. That was strange. She must have bolted as soon as Beach told them they had the rest of the day off. Johnny scanned the beach, but the only blondes he saw wore flashy bikinis, not a one-piece blue suit.

He gazed back toward the hotel and pool. His eyes locked on the storage shed. There she was. Her back was to him. She leaned against the shed as if she was getting sick. A flash of alarm went through him. He rushed over to her.

"Kylie?"

She didn't turn around. She was trembling, he noticed.

She was sobbing.

"Hey, come on," Johnny said softly. At first he didn't dare, but then he reached out and touched her shoulder. "Are you okay?"

Kylie whirled on him, wrapping her arms around his shoulders and pulling him close. Tears streaked down her face, and her eyes were full of fear and exhaustion.

Johnny did the only thing he could do. He hugged her back.

"It's okay, Ky," he whispered. "We did it. We saved him. Everything is okay now."

"N-No, it's not!" she said, voice hitching. "A man almost died today, Johnny. If we hadn't . . . he'd be dead right now! He *was* dead! He wasn't breathing. He had no pulse. The man was *dead!*"

A lump formed in Johnny's throat, but still he smiled. "But he's not dead, Kylie. We saved him. It's what we're trained for. It's our job, and today we proved how good we are. We did great." He took a deep breath to fight off his own emotions. "We're a great team."

Kylie pulled him closer. "It was so close, Johnny. He was so close to—"

"I know," he whispered. "I know."

Kylie pulled back slightly, looking into Johnny's eyes.

Johnny held her gaze for a moment. Then they mutually pulled back and broke the embrace. "You going to be okay?" he asked.

"I guess so," Kylie replied, letting out a deep sigh. "It's just so scary."

Johnny nodded. They didn't speak for a moment. Kylie stared out at the white-capped water, her eyes distant; she seemed to be replaying mental videotape. "Maybe it was a bad idea to come down here by myself."

He didn't know what she meant. Down here by the storage shed?

"Kylie?" he said.

"I mean, to Surf City," she explained. "I wanted sort of a safe trial run of living on my own, away from my family, so I scanned the summer shares ads and found a bungalow just off the boardwalk with two girls looking for a third roommate. The rent was so cheap, and the girls are nice and all, but we're really just acquaintances. Plus they work in restaurants, so I don't know that they'd even understand what today was like—"

Kylie broke off as a sob overtook her. "I just feel . . . so all alone." She covered her face with her hands. "You must think I'm such a baby."

Johnny offered a smile. "I don't think a baby could have told Tanner he was an idiot or performed mouth-to-mouth under pressure."

She took her hands away from her face and sniffled.

Johnny felt like his heart would break. He had to make her feel better. "Hey, I have an idea."

Kylie sniffled again, her eyes on the ground. "Yeah?"

"We have the whole afternoon off," Johnny pointed out. "And what we both need after today is to get away from the beach. Get away from Surf City, even. We could have a celebratory dinner or something. What do you say?"

Kylie seemed to contemplate this for a moment.

Bad idea, he thought. *She wants no part of today's memory, at least for now. Dumb suggestion. Just go home and—*

"Okay," Kylie whispered.

Johnny cocked an eyebrow. "Yeah?"

Kylie wiped away a tear and smiled. "Yeah."

The plan was to take an hour and a half to clean up, get dressed, and get their heart rates back to normal. Then Johnny would pick her up, and they'd head down the coast to a cute resort town about twenty miles from Surf City. Johnny had felt oddly protective of Kylie as he watched her bike away toward her bungalow; he'd wanted to run after her and make sure she could pedal the half mile okay. After what she'd been through—what they'd both been through together—he figured it was all right for him to be concerned. Plus there was no one else down here who cared about her.

Johnny took his time showering away the sweat and sunblock, then delved into Danny's music collection to help himself relax as he got dressed. He told himself not to think about Harold and what had happened today. He ordered himself not to think about Kylie. The music helped him chill out and free his mind. By the time he needed to leave, Johnny felt in control again.

He backed his cherry red Jeep out of the apartment house's parking lot for the first time since June, grateful for the opportunity to drive. He and his brothers walked or biked everywhere in Surf City, and Johnny had never felt the need to take off down the coast with the top down, the wind in his hair. Never until today.

He'd pulled an unconscious man out of the water this afternoon. Something that required instant reaction. Logic and thought had very little to do with it. Training and the pure gut instinct to *save* simply took over. Johnny had never been in that position before, and he'd certainly never felt anything like it before. If he'd spent even a moment mentally going over what he needed to do and in what order and whether or not he was truly up to the task, Harold O'Hearn could have died.

The sight of Kylie leaning against her dark blue car—a Ford, no less—in jeans and a tank top almost took his breath away. It certainly took away any thought of drowning victims and emergency rescues. He pulled in the driveway of her bungalow, and she hopped in, offering him a smile. In minutes they were driving south down the coast in companionable silence. The kind of silence that felt right instead of awkward. The kind of silence during which nothing needed to be said.

The sun had begun its daily plunge into the sea. The dinner hour would be at hand. *Perfect timing,* Johnny thought with a smile. He had to admit it was strange seeing Kylie fully dressed. Her honey blond hair fell to her shoulders, not pulled back like when she was on duty. He noticed a light dusting of makeup on her face, around her amazing blue-green eyes and on her pink lips. Her white tank top accentuated her tan, and she wore denim capris and sandals. The blue dolphins continued their endless journey around her ankle.

"Where are we going?" she asked.

"A fish joint on Hannibal Bay," Johnny replied. "Great oysters."

Kylie smiled. "I *love* oysters."

"Whew," Johnny replied. "Not many people do."

"I ate them ever since I was a kid," she said, eyes scanning the passing landscape. "My parents thought I was weird." Then she looked at him. "What would you have done if I didn't like oysters?"

Johnny shrugged. "Recommended the french fries."

Six

THE PLACE WAS called Zeppe's. It was a roadhouse-style joint that sat right on the water of Hannibal Bay. A sawdust-on-the-floor, blues-in-the-juke kind of place. Zeppe's specialized in seafood: oysters, crabs, lobster, the works. The smell of Old Bay seasoning was spread throughout the room by a team of ceiling fans. The windows faced west to let in the golden blood of the sunset, but Johnny and Kylie took a table on the deck outside. On a piling out on the water, a pelican watched them lazily.

"After this summer," Johnny said, scowling and sipping his soda, "I don't think I'll ever have another Fizz Cola."

Kylie laughed. "I've been off the stuff ever since I caught my ex with Miss Fizz."

Johnny smiled, surprised yet again by Kylie's personality. Despite everything she'd been through, her sense of humor was still intact—even at her own expense. He learned more and more about this girl each day. Each minute, even.

"But what happens if you win the volleyball tournament?" Kylie asked. "You'll be up to your eyeballs in Fizz Cola."

"I'll sell it on eBay," Johnny replied, wiggling his eyebrows. "But like you said that first day we were partnered—it's not *if* we win the tournament. It's *when*."

Kylie shot him a grin as she sipped a club soda. "Of course. How could I forget?"

"I'm serious," Johnny replied. "If we don't win, this whole summer will be a bust. It's the whole reason Danny, Kevin, and I came to Surf City. That ten K in prize money is a nice score. I need it for school."

"I know what you mean," Kylie agreed. "I've been stashing away as much as I possibly can this summer."

"You put it in a savings account?"

Kylie nodded.

"If you have enough dough to open one, I'd suggest putting it in a money-market mutual fund. At the very least. A stock fund would be better. You're probably only getting one-point-eight percent interest from the bank. A money-market fund bumps you up to five percent. Then the interest compounds. It makes a big difference."

"Let me guess," Kylie said drolly. "Finance major?"

Johnny laughed. "Money major."

"Well, my portfolio is pretty sparse right now,"

Kylie replied, swizzling her drink. "Lifeguards don't exactly rake it in."

"We should," Johnny replied. "After what we pulled off today."

Kylie nodded but didn't reply.

"I don't want to belabor it," Johnny said gently. "But you were pretty freaked out today. You all right?"

Again she nodded, her eyes distant. "I'll never forget that feeling, Johnny. Never. How there was absolutely no life in that man's body. It was terrifying. Life is so short. I mean, Mr. O'Hearn has to be seventy, and I bet he was thinking how seventy years just went by in a blink—how could it be over now?" She sighed. "You just never know."

A shiver went through Johnny. He tried not to show it. "All I kept thinking was, 'What if he dies? What if we can't revive him?' I don't know what I would've done. I mean, we had the man's life in our hands. We were his one shot. What if we screwed up?"

"I guess that's the whole point of taking risks, though, isn't it?" She tilted her head, thinking for a moment. "I mean, people have probably told Mr. O'Hearn he's too old to be frolicking in the ocean. But if he'd listened, he wouldn't have had the joy of swimming in the Pacific, you know? A hard wave could catch anyone off guard. Could you imagine not going swimming just because you might get a mouthful of water or knocked around by a wave?"

"I guess it's like being a lifeguard too," Johnny said. "If we were too afraid of the possibility of having to rescue someone, we'd miss out on how it feels to help people, to actually save a life."

Kylie nodded. "It was the scariest thing I've ever faced, but I wouldn't trade the job."

"Me either."

Kylie looked out over the water to the setting sun. "You know, you called this a celebratory dinner, and that's what it should be. A celebration. We shouldn't be moaning about how scared we were. We should be celebrating that Mr. O'Hearn's okay, that we saved his life. Which means, I think we deserve more oysters."

Johnny smiled and signaled the waiter. "So, how about we change the subject, to something we're both psyched about. Allman."

Kylie beamed. "I can't wait! I can't wait to live in a dorm, meet my roommate, eat bad cafeteria food every meal, pull all-nighters, be exposed to so many different people, things, ideas—"

"Wow," Johnny said. "You are into it. I am too, but I guess I wasn't even looking at it like you are. The exposure to new things, I mean. I always figured college was about hard work. Studying to get good grades so you never take for granted you're there. I'm the first person in our family to go to college."

"I didn't know that," Kylie said. "I can see why you'd look at college as a privilege, then. I think that's really nice."

"So you're definitely majoring in psych?"

Kylie nodded, a twinkle gleaming in her eye. "Is it true that guys ask girls what their major is as a line? When I visited Allman, some of the girls said if a guy asks you what your major is, it's the first in a long series of lines meant to get you back to his dorm room."

"I have absolutely no idea," Johnny said. "I've had a girlfriend for so long that I wouldn't even know how to use a line on the opposite sex."

Jane, he said mentally. This was the first time all day that he'd even *thought* of her. After what he'd been through, it made no sense that he didn't call Jane at the first opportunity to tell her about it, share his news, be comforted by her concern. But it had never even occurred to him to call her. He waited for the anticipated emotion to punish him but then realized it wasn't coming. He didn't feel guilty. He didn't know why, but guilt wasn't even a blip on his radar screen at the moment. All he felt was positive energy.

Kylie looked him right in the eye. "I don't think you'd ever need to use a line, Johnny Ford. I think you could have any girl you wanted just by smiling at her."

His cheeks didn't start burning. He didn't sheepishly glance down. He didn't rush to change the subject out of secretly pleased embarrassment.

He simply smiled at her.

They ate nearly two dozen oysters and two shrimp cocktails between them. Johnny now had the pleasant burn of Tabasco and cocktail sauce at the corners of his mouth. He did, however, switch from Fizz to water. Soda and oysters just didn't go.

The conversation swayed from subject to subject, never returning to the events of the afternoon. It still hovered clear in Johnny's mind, but Kylie seemed to be having such a good time that he let it alone. But there was another subject that they hadn't discussed, and Johnny was wondering if he'd spoil an otherwise great moment by bringing it up.

"So what really happened between you and Jane?" he asked, regretting it the moment it was out of his mouth. "I mean, the whole story, not the short form about cheerleading and a guy."

Kylie's blue-green eyes locked on his. "Are you asking because you feel guilty about being here with me?"

Johnny cocked an eyebrow. He'd never said the girl wasn't direct. "No. I don't feel guilty. Though maybe I should feel guilty for *not* feeling guilty. Anyway, let's leave the present out of it. What happened in the past, Kylie? What was so horrible and terrible and awful?"

Kylie sighed. "You asked. Just remember that."

Johnny nodded.

"Okay," she said, tucking a strand of her honey-colored hair behind her ear. "Here goes. Cheerleading tryouts, seventh grade. Jane and I practiced together all the time. Before school, during lunch, till dinner, and then after dinner till curfew. We wanted it so bad that we believed we'd make it—together. It had never occurred to either one of us that only one of us might get chosen."

"Ah," Johnny said. "And only one of you did."

Kylie nodded. "Me."

"Well, that wouldn't make Jane hate you for life," Johnny commented. "It gets worse, I assume?"

"Much," Kylie said, taking a sip of club soda. "Jane was devastated. She wanted me to turn down my spot on the squad in the name of our friendship, but I didn't want to. I was upset that she even asked it of me. So, she got angry and started accusing me of sucking up to the judges behind her back. And then she sought her revenge."

Johnny raised an eyebrow. "Which was . . . ?"

Kylie sighed. "She stole Larry Finkel away from me."

Johnny's mouth fell open. "Larry Finkel? Um, didn't he get unofficially named Class Geek?"

Kylie smiled. "Yeah, but back in seventh grade, he was the hottest thing at Spring Valley Central Middle School. Every girl wanted him. He didn't turn nerd until he hit puberty. Anyway, I was madly in love with Larry. He was the first boy I ever kissed. And he asked me to be his girlfriend right before Valentine's Day. I was beyond thrilled. I spent hours picking out just the right card and just the right CD with my baby-sitting money."

Johnny took a sip of his soda. "Uh-oh. Where does Jane come in?"

"Well, at school on Valentine's Day, Larry was waiting for me at my locker—I thought to give me a card and present. But no. He dumped me. He told me he'd fallen for another girl over the week-end. Later I saw him and Jane walking down the hall, holding hands. She carried a red rose all day.

They even stopped right in front of me and kissed—a *long* kiss."

"That doesn't sound like Larry," Johnny pointed out. "He was one of the nicest guys at Spring Valley High."

"Don't blame him," Kylie said. "Jane had told him horrible lies about me. Since we used to be friends, she knew enough stuff about my life to make up great ones that sounded believable enough. Stupid stuff, but stories that would turn off a very nice guy like Larry. He never looked at me again."

Johnny shook his head. "It's a good thing I went to a different middle school. This kind of junior-high bull would have turned my stomach."

"Oh, I'm hardly done," she admitted. "It gets *much* worse."

"Spill," Johnny said, not sure he could take any more. It was hard to hear that his girlfriend was the bad guy in the cold war. But he'd asked, so he had to hear Kylie out.

"Well, I went totally intercontinental ballistic missile on Jane," Kylie continued. "It was war as far as I was concerned. I did everything I could to make her life miserable. I started by sabotaging her locker with molasses."

"Good one," Johnny said.

"I thought so," Kylie replied. "But I wished I'd stopped at that. Because that was what sparked the real war. We went back and forth, each thing worse than the next. She stole my gym clothes. I stole her homework. But I knew that no matter what I did, she had Larry. So I did the worst thing I could think of—something that would nuke her entire existence at Spring Valley Central."

Johnny leaned forward, bracing himself and dying to know at the same time.

Kylie took a deep breath. "I started a rumor that Jane had sex. That she'd been able to steal Larry from me because she told him she'd have sex with him and that they did it every day in the basement of his house and sometimes behind the Dumpster at school."

Johnny narrowed his eyes, immediately sympathizing with Jane. He was also sort of relieved that his girlfriend *wasn't* the only bad guy.

Kylie nodded. "Everyone believed it. Larry swore up and down that it wasn't true, but no one believed him. They thought he was just Nice Larry, trying to save his girlfriend's rep. After a while he couldn't deal with the fact that everyone thought his girlfriend was a slut. I mean, a girl *didn't* have sex in seventh grade, you know?"

He knew. If a guy was rumored to be doing it in seventh grade, his stock went through the roof into stud territory. But a girl? She went directly to slut. "I think I'm starting to see the big picture here."

"It gets worse," Kylie said, shooting him a weak smile.

Johnny stared at her. "You're kidding."

"'Fraid not," she said, sipping her club soda. "After Larry dumped her, every guy asked Jane out because they thought she'd sleep with them. She didn't go out with one guy all year—in eighth grade either. The rumors had died down by then, of course, but Jane could never be sure if a guy liked her for her or because of the rumors. By the time we all started at Spring Valley High, Jane's rep had pretty much turned—she was considered an ice princess who never dated."

Johnny shook his head. "Until me."

"Until you," Kylie confirmed. "Clearly *you* liked her for real. For three years running. I'll bet you gave her back her confidence in that department. I mean, her ability to believe that a guy wants her for her."

Johnny was suddenly consumed with tenderness for Jane. He wished he could send her a giant bear hug four hours up the coast. He wondered if what she'd gone through had helped shape her, make her all serious and guarded. He was sure it had.

"I really regret what I did," Kylie said. "At the time it seemed justified. It wasn't my fault that I got chosen for cheerleading. She told my boyfriend horrible lies about me and then stole him. I wanted to totally destroy her! But I never meant to hurt her that badly."

"It's a terrible story," Johnny agreed. "But it's not like her rep followed her to high school. I certainly never heard about it."

"Jane will probably never forget it," Kylie said, her eyes downcast.

"Did you ever apologize?"

"No," Kylie answered. "In fact, I never publicly

admitted starting the rumor. But Jane knew it was me. No one else had a reason to be so cruel."

Johnny frowned, letting the whole sordid story sink in. So much more made sense now. Of course Jane would hate Kylie. And of course Jane would worry that Kylie would take the opportunity to steal her boyfriend away again. Even if they'd already one-upped each other a long time ago.

"Thanks, Kylie," Johnny said, looking her in the eye.

"For what?"

"For telling me the truth," he said. "I can understand why neither of you wanted to share the dirty details."

Kylie leaned back in her chair. "Hate me now too?"

Johnny looked at her. "Of course not. The story's worse than I ever imagined, but it's junior-high immaturity gone really awry. She hurt you, you hurt her, she hurt you, you hurt her. And she just happened to have the last hurt. I guess I understand why she held on to the grudge, but I also think the whole thing is stupid."

"Jane didn't have the last hurt," Kylie corrected him. "She might have thought so, but she got me back."

Johnny was confused. "How?"

"Maybe I'll tell you one day," Kylie said, glancing out the window. "Right now, I think I've told you more than enough."

Johnny nodded. "You're right."

She smiled. "Anyway, we're supposed to be celebrating."

"Let's get out of here," he suggested. He suddenly needed fresh air, the smell of the ocean, and a good, long walk to let everything—this whole day—sink in.

"Time to go home?" she asked.

"No."

She let out a breath he didn't even know she was holding. "Good."

Seven

JOHNNY AND KYLIE got some ice cream and strolled down a long dock out over the bay. They didn't talk much. They just ate their cones and enjoyed the moment.

A sudden blast of light over the bay made Johnny jump. Red and white sparks drizzled down, followed by a loud explosion.

"Fireworks!" Kylie exclaimed. "Cool."

"What's the occasion?" Johnny wondered.

"Us saving Mr. O'Hearn!" Kylie exclaimed, flashing him a smile.

More rockets popped off, sending glares across the bay. Hardly anyone was around on the dock. They had the best seats in the house all to themselves.

He was suddenly aware of Kylie moving closer. Her arm brushing his.

Johnny dared to look at her. A massive white bloom illuminated her face. She was staring back at him.

"Johnny?" she asked softly.

His throat was tight. He felt the pounding of his pulse throughout his body. "Yeah?"

Kylie blinked; she didn't say anything. As if she wanted to say something, but suddenly couldn't.

"I—," he began

She stepped toward him. *Is she going to kiss me?* he wondered in a panic. But before she could come closer, before she could do what Johnny wanted her to do more than anything in the world, he pulled away.

"I'm sorry, Kylie," he whispered, his voice choked with regret. "But I can't. I can't do this." He wasn't sure what else to say. He wanted to apologize, he wanted to scream, he wanted to tell Kylie that even though he wouldn't kiss her, he wanted to. Like crazy.

You knew it was coming to this, the voice in his head warned. *You knew you were attracted to her from day one. You can't just bury those feelings. You have to face what you know: You may love Jane, but after today's rescue you and Kylie have an emotional bond that not many people experience. A bond that may well be worth something other than a summer fling.*

What? What was his conscience telling him? That Kylie was the one? No. He wouldn't accept that. It was too easy to be with Kylie. She was fun. Funny. Down-to-earth. Dialed in to the same frequencies as Johnny. But most of all, she was here, now. Jane was far away. Just because there were miles between them didn't mean that Johnny didn't still care for her.

Miles, Johnny mused. *Now, there's an understatement.*

But he knew these pathetic excuses didn't mean anything. He was with Jane. End of story.

The fireworks pounded the sky above them, shooting rays of light across the water, across their faces.

"Kylie, I—"

"Don't," she cut him off, holding up a hand. "I know the score, Johnny. I shouldn't have done that."

"It's okay, Kylie."

She shook her head. "It's not okay. Especially after the story I just told you. It's very not okay." She turned away for a moment, covering her face with her hands. "It's just that . . . today was really hard. And you were so great. And I don't just mean with Mr. O'Hearn. I mean with me. The dinner, the conversations, the fireworks, all of it. Even now, when I tried to kiss you . . . you did the right thing."

Johnny put a hand on her shoulder. "Kylie, don't beat yourself up, okay? I'm here with you, aren't I? I'm not exactly king of 'doing the right thing.'"

Kylie nodded, sniffing. "Maybe we should go, huh?"

"Good idea," Johnny said.

They walked in silence along the dock as the fireworks finished above them. Streaks of red, white, and blue flashed along the ground, scattering their shadows left and right.

The sparks and booms faded behind them as they drove north in silence.

★   ★   ★

You were so close, Johnny thought.

He stared out from his apartment balcony, three stories above the Surf City boardwalk. He lounged in a kitchen chair, his feet propped on the railing. A cool breeze cut across his bare torso, wisping the hairs on his chest.

Close to what? Kissing a girl he couldn't get out of his mind? A girl who challenged him, surprised him, made him think, made him . . . want to kiss her so bad, he couldn't breathe?

But another girl is coming to town in three days, he reminded himself. *And she's the one you love.*

He *had* cheated on Jane. He had been with Kylie. The feelings were there too. They still were. This wasn't some court case to be argued by a slick lawyer. Intent to cheat was just as bad as cheating. And he had intended for something to happen when he suggested they have a celebratory dinner. Maybe just intimate conversation, like they'd had. But that was enough for cheating. The whole day had been leading to a kiss.

If so, then why didn't you go through with it? the voice demanded. *You could've kissed Kylie silly and still have been just as guilty.*

Because Jane was his girlfriend, that's why. He loved her. The state of their relationship hadn't been an issue with him all summer because there was no reason for it to be. Jane and Johnny. Class Couple. Girlfriend-boyfriend. Black and white. As certain and final as a winning point in volleyball.

So lay off, conscience, Johnny ordered, heading

back inside. *I've got enough on my mind as it is.*

Kevin and Penny were on the couch. Kevin sat; Penny lay sprawled out, her feet on his lap. Kevin was giving her a foot massage. Danny and Raven were out, trying to scam tickets for some punk band called I Love Portia de Rossi.

"How was your date?" Kevin asked, his eyes glued to *Felicity* on the television.

Johnny dropped down in the recliner. "Date? Don't get what you mean, little bro."

Kevin and Penny exchanged glances. "You and Kylie spent the evening together, right? You spend all day together, right? Am I wrong in thinking there's something brewing here?"

Johnny turned up the volume on the TV by remote, but the thing wasn't working. "Couldn't be more wrong, dude. Of course Kylie and I spent the day together—we're coworkers. Partners. And I told you when I walked in—Beach gave us the rest of the afternoon off, so we took a drive to let off steam and had some dinner. No big deal."

Again Kevin and Penny exchanged looks. "Not to be poops about it, Johnny," Kevin said. "But we don't believe you."

Johnny rolled his eyes. "What's there to believe? That I'm messing around on my girlfriend? That just because I work with someone who's vaguely attractive and in a bathing suit all day, I have to be having an affair with her?"

"Vaguely attractive?" Penny asked incredulously. "Kylie's beautiful."

"So what?" Johnny muttered. He banged the remote on the recliner to make it work.

Kevin and Penny burst out laughing. "You owe me a buck," Kevin said to her.

Penny slid a hand in her pocket and flipped Kevin a crumpled single. "And I had so much faith." She shook her head.

"What's this?" Johnny demanded. "What are you two talking about?"

Kevin grinned, snapping open his dollar. "We had a bet. I said you'd hook up with Kylie. But Penny took the high road. She thought you'd hold out."

Anger rolled through Johnny. "Then you better cough up, little brother. Because *nothing* happened."

"No way," Kevin chided. "You caved. It's all over your face."

"Nope," Johnny said flatly. "I was presented with a test and, as always, I passed with flying colors."

"Ha! We were right!" Kevin exclaimed, pointing at Johnny with Penny's foot. "I knew something would happen between you and Kylie. I knew it!" He leaned forward. "So what did happen?"

Penny sat up. "You're worse than a girl, Kevin. Leave him alone."

"Don't give me that, Pen," Kevin replied. "You're just as curious."

Johnny sighed, rubbing his temples. He told himself he was only going to share the day's and night's events with them to get them off his back. But he knew deep down he was going to tell because he needed to talk to someone, anyone, about it. Was he really wrong?

"It was no big deal," he began. He told them about Kylie crying at the shed, about his offer to get out of town for a little while. About how he and Kylie talked about everything—including the truth behind the war with Jane. He finished with the scene on the dock and the kiss that wasn't.

"Johnny, I don't know why you're tearing yourself apart over this," Penny said. She ran a hand through her short, brown hair. "You didn't do anything wrong. Forging a bond with someone you work with is inevitable, especially after what you went through on the beach today. But you stayed true to Jane. Not because it was the right thing to do. But because you wanted to stay faithful to her."

"Yeah, what she said," Kevin added, gesturing at Penny.

Johnny shook his head. "No. I wanted to kiss her."

Penny and Kevin shared a look but didn't say anything.

"I wanted to kiss her," Johnny went on, "but I didn't. Either way, I cheated on Jane because I have genuine feelings for someone else."

"Johnny, you didn't—," Penny began.

"Penny, let's say Kevin had the chance to make out with some girl behind a palm tree near the pool but didn't out of *guilt,* not because he wasn't into it. As his girlfriend, how would that make you feel?"

Penny slumped deeper into the couch. "I see your point."

"That *never* happened, by the way," Kevin said, grinning.

"So," Johnny said. "I'm a jerk. I have to figure out what to do about Kylie—because we still have to work together. And then I have to figure out what I'm going to tell—or not tell—Jane."

As if on cue, the phone rang.

All three of them stared at the cordless on the coffee table as if it was radioactive. They all knew who was on the other end. They all knew what would happen if one of them answered it.

It rang again. Loud as a scream.

Kevin chuckled. "Well, bro, better break out the calculator. Because all your figuring is about to take place right now."

Eight

"So I PULLED him out of the water," Johnny said, "and a few other lifeguards helped lay him onto the sand."

Jane sucked in a breath on the other end of the telephone. "Wow, Johnny. You must have been so freaked out! Then what happened?"

"So, um, I did chest compressions, and, um, one of the other lifeguards did mouth-to-mouth."

Out of the corner of his eye Johnny noticed Kevin staring at him intensely, shaking his head very slowly and mouthing the words *don't tell*. Penny was trying to cover Kevin's mouth with her hand.

"I'm surprised it wasn't Kylie who did the mouth-to-mouth," Jane said, followed by a sharp, mean laugh. "She'd kiss anyone for attention."

Johnny froze, then shot up off the recliner and walked into the kitchen for a little more privacy. As he leaned against the refrigerator, a hot wave of anger hit him flat in the belly. Kylie had saved a man's life today. And that was nothing to poke fun at. "Actually, it *was* Kylie who did the mouth-to-mouth. She saved Harold O'Hearn as much as I did."

Dead silence.

"Jane?"

More silence.

"Jane, c'mon," Johnny said, his voice clipped. "She's my partner. Of course we performed CPR together."

Kevin appeared in the open doorway to the kitchen, waving his hands frantically in the air, in a stop-now-or-you're-dead-meat gesture. Johnny turned around, facing the tiny window—and whatever other questions or comments Jane might hit him with.

"So then what happened?" Jane asked coldly. "Back to work, business as usual? I guess you and Kylie probably talked about what happened all day long."

"Well, actually," Johnny began, "Beach gave us the rest of the day off. A rescue like that can really take everything out of you, so we wouldn't have been as focused as we'd have to be."

"Oh, so what did you do with the free after-noon?" Jane asked, sounding more relaxed. "Walked along the boardwalk? I know how you like to take long walks when you've got something on your mind."

Johnny hadn't taken a long walk since he'd ar-rived in Surf City. He hadn't needed to. Something about the sun, the sound of the waves, the whole attitude, and maybe even having his brothers around calmed him down.

But what was he supposed to tell Jane? That he spent his afternoon off with Kylie? That he suggested dinner? That they'd shared oysters and talked about the most intimate details of Jane's life as a thirteen-year-old and then almost kissed on the dock?

Johnny ran a hand through his hair. He had to cop out. At the moment that was all he could handle. "Jane, I'm really exhausted after today. I think I need to go lie down and take a nap." *Or just get off the phone so I don't have to deal with this,* he added mentally. He winced at the way he was treating her. Granted, she was being a little hostile, but he understood why.

Better than ever, actually. *Hey, everyone, Jane Jarvis had sex with Larry Finkel behind the Dumpster!* He envisioned thirteen-year-old Jane, serious, nononsense Jane, confused and scared and devastated over a lie. A lie that had serious consequences to her social life, her self-esteem—everything.

But Jane started it, a weak voice intruded. If she hadn't stolen Larry Finkel from Kylie, Kylie wouldn't have put molasses in Jane's locker, and Jane wouldn't have stolen Kylie's homework, and Kylie wouldn't have started one very vicious rumor.

"Why don't we change the subject?" she suggested. "You can ask about my day."

"Jane, I'm really wiped, okay?"

"Is Kylie as tired and grumpy as you are?" Jane snapped.

"I don't know," he snapped back. "And if I did, I probably wouldn't tell you."

Silence. "Why not?"

"Because you hate her guts, that's why," Johnny pointed out. "And the girl is my partner, okay? I have to work with her."

Jane sighed. "I'm sorry, Johnny. I know you didn't pick her as your partner or anything. Actually, I should feel very bad for you."

"Why?"

"For being stuck working with that lying, cheating monster. I don't know how you stand it."

"Jane . . ."

"Oh, wait a minute," Jane began, "I forgot. She probably put on her sweet act. She probably cried today after you guys rescued that man. 'Oh, Johnny, it was so scary! Oh, Johnny, he almost died! Hold me, Johnny, hold me and make all the bad memories go away!' She pulled that, didn't she?"

Johnny's mouth dropped open. Kylie had sort of done exactly what Jane had just described.

"All right, I'm making you mad," Jane said. "I know you're angry when you get quiet. I'm sorry. But listen to me, Johnny. Kylie is *not* the nice person she's probably making herself out to be. She's vicious."

"Jane, you've been telling me that since we met, but you've never told me why you hate her so much. All you say is 'cheerleading and a guy.' That makes it sound like it wasn't a very big deal."

A pause. "Well, trust me—it was."

He wanted, *needed* to hear the story from Jane's lips. He needed her to reinforce the trust between them, the intimacy they'd spent three years developing. Maybe then she'd knock Kylie out of his mind. *Maybe*. "So tell me. Tell me what happened."

Another pause. "I can't."

Johnny sighed. "Why not?"

"Because I just can't," Jane said. "It brings back a lot of bad memories, and if I start talking about it, I'll cry. And then it'll be on my mind, and I'll feel like that thirteen-year-old girl all over again. I never want to relive that, Johnny, okay?"

"Maybe talking about it will finally get it out of you," Johnny pointed out. "Maybe you'll finally be able to forget all about it."

"Well, it's no surprise that Kylie hasn't told you the whole horrible story," Jane said.

Johnny swallowed.

"Because if she told you what she did to me," Jane continued, "you'd hate her too. You'd never be able to even look at her again, and she knows that. Her I'm-so-sweet act would be ruined."

Johnny closed his eyes, feeling like all the blood had drained out of him. "Jane, I want to make something very, very clear, okay?"

"Okay," she said hesitantly.

"I love you," he told her. "We've been together for three years. We've been through everything together. I would never, ever do anything to hurt you."

There was dead silence on the other end, as if Jane was waiting for the ball to drop.

"But you *did*—is that it?" she asked. He could feel her heart squeezing on the other end.

"Kylie told me what happened," he admitted. "She told me everything. And it didn't make me hate her."

"What!" Jane's voice rose an octave. "I want to know what she said."

"Jane, look—I understand why you hate her. I honestly do. But in the context of everything she said, and how long ago it was, and the person she seems to be now—"

"Johnny, I want to know what she told you," Jane snapped.

"I thought you didn't want to talk about it."

"I don't," she said, her voice growing edgier. "But I want to know what my worst enemy is telling my boyfriend about me. She probably told you a long list of lies."

"Let's just drop it," he said. "I'm tired of the Kylie argument. I've had a wicked day, and I just want to go to sleep."

"This isn't right, Johnny. Kylie's the worst kind of manipulator. She's working some scam, I'm sure of it. Don't listen to her."

"Jane, can't we please just let it go? I'm so beat. After the day I've had, please?"

"Johnny, we shouldn't leave it like this."

"We'll talk tomorrow, okay?"

"Johnny . . . I love you too."

He swallowed hard. "I know. And you know I love you."

He said good night and clicked the phone dead. His hand dropped from his ear into his lap. He closed his eyes.

What was he going to do? He *did* love Jane. They *did* have three years together. She was his girlfriend. Of course he loved her.

Of course I love her, he echoed mentally.

So why do I have feelings for another girl?

Kevin's voice came from the couch: "Can't wait till Jane gets here, bro! You're dead meat!"

The beach was still there the next day.

Johnny showed up for work a bit early, hoping to get settled and be staring out at the water when Kylie arrived. That way he could simply keep his eyes on the Pacific—and away from her.

"Hi," she said as she climbed up next to him.

"Hey," he replied.

He didn't move a muscle as she took her seat and stretched out her long, tanned legs. He could smell that amazing cocoa-butter lotion.

"Funny weather today, huh?" she commented.

Johnny nodded. Whitecaps danced on the waves, torn across the sea by a stiff wind. A rainbow of colored sails dotted the horizon, their pilots taking full advantage of the sunny yet argumentative weather. Swimmers were scattered. The waves were rough, sending most of the beach bums to the pool and calmer waters. Johnny was grateful for the sailboats. At least he had something to stare at.

"I think I'll do a patrol up and down the shoreline," Kylie said, hopping up. She climbed down to the sand. "See you in a few."

Johnny let out a deep breath as he watched her jog to the surf, then walk south. She stopped to help a little girl put her nose plug back on properly, then resumed patrol.

He was grateful for the time alone. He could see her, her figure outlined in the sun, her blond hair shining, the white lifeguard patch on the back of her bathing suit, but she was far enough away so that he could attempt to sort through his thoughts.

An hour later he hadn't gotten very far. Not past: *I definitely have feelings for the girl. And my girlfriend, who I claim to love, will be here in mere days.*

Kylie jogged up to the chair and climbed next to him. "No problems," she said, a bit stiffly. "Although a little boy dove into a wave and came up for air minus his swimming trunks."

That was Kylie. Offering an icebreaker. Once again she'd forced Johnny to smile when he didn't want to. "How are you?" he asked carefully.

Kylie chuckled. "At last he speaks."

Johnny chuckled too. "You weren't exactly breaking land speech records before you bolted for beach patrol."

"Maybe I was trying to figure out what to say." Kylie leaned back and rested her elbows on the back of the chair. "Things got kinda intense last night."

Intense? That was an understatement, as far as he was concerned. "I know."

"Don't hate me for last night, Johnny. I'm sorry I put you on the spot."

"Any guy would kill for the spot you put me on last night."

She looked into his eyes for a moment, then glanced down at her toes. "It was just a really wild day."

"I know." He nodded, glancing at her. "Kylie, I have a girlfriend."

"Really?" she asked, looking at him like he was crazy. "I had no idea."

Johnny took a deep breath. "What I mean is, the problems between you and Jane aren't the issue. The *issue* is that I have a girlfriend, and I almost kissed you last night."

"So you did want to kiss me," she said, turning to face him.

He locked eyes with her. He saw everything in those green-blue depths. A past he wanted to know, a present he wanted to explore, a future he wanted to be a part of. "Yes, I did," he confirmed. "I'm not proud of it."

"I wasn't sure if I'd made a total fool of myself or not," Kylie said softly. "After telling you all about how Jane stole Larry Finkel from me, there I was, trying to steal you from her."

"So Jane's right," he said weakly.

Kylie reached behind her head to tighten her ponytail. "She thinks I'm trying to steal you from her?"

"Yup."

"I didn't intend to," Kylie said. "You're taken, and I respect that. I just—"

"Just what?" he prodded, nervous about the territory they were in.

"I just . . . got to know you better than I ever figured I would, I guess. And that took care of that."

"I know what you mean," he responded, staring out at the water. He watched a wind surfer skip across the waves about fifty yards out. The breeze blew static in his ears.

"You do?" she whispered. She reached out her hand to gently turn his chin to face her. He stared into her eyes and saw the same confusion and longing he knew were reflected in his.

All Johnny could manage in response was a nod. He turned away, and she released her hand.

"Johnny?"

"I think we should just focus on the job today, Kylie. And not talk about this anymore. At least for now, okay?"

"Okay," she said, twirling her whistle.

Johnny released a deep breath as Kevin's words came rushing into his head. The kid had been right.

Johnny was dead meat.

True to their word, they hadn't talked about their "situation" for the rest of the day. They'd barely spoken, as a matter of fact. Kylie had done another beach patrol in both directions of their stretch. Johnny had stood up and yelled at kids to stay within the boundaries more times than he actually spoke to Kylie.

"Four o'clock," Kylie announced, standing up and slipping on her cutoffs. "Quitting time." She threw her gear down to the sand.

"Kylie—"

She turned to face him, waiting.

But Johnny had absolutely nothing to say. He couldn't bear to let her go, but he couldn't very well suggest they go off for an evening of fun either. He'd spent the past few hours thinking about stuff—not about their situation, but about himself. The person he was, the way he was. He wished he could talk to her about it, get her perspective. It wasn't like he could talk to his brothers, and Jane wouldn't understand what his problem was.

Kylie would, though.

"Johnny, I have an idea," she said. "We can't work together if we're uncomfortable around each other, if we're not friends who talk, right?"

He nodded. "Today was pretty tough."

"So, why don't we just accept the fact that we enjoy each other's company and be friends? There's nothing so terrible about that, Johnny."

"So no talking about Jane, no talking about us?" Johnny asked.

"None at all," she said.

Johnny grinned. "I know the *best* pizza place."

She grinned back. "I'm dying for a gooey slice."

They climbed down, locked their gear in the

shed, slipped on T-shirts and their shoes, and then strolled down the boardwalk. The familiar sights and smells came at them from all angles: fried food, squeals of delight, the backbeat of rap music, the roar of the roller coaster on the pier. Johnny was so used to these things that he hardly sensed them anymore. Like a country boy becoming desensitized to the big city.

They found a booth at Pope's Pizza, Johnny's favorite, an old-fashioned pizza joint with checkered tablecloths and paper place mats. They ordered two slices and two sodas each.

"I wonder if I'm too grown-up for my own good," Johnny said as the teenage waiter flipped shut his order pad and headed toward the kitchen. That was what he'd been thinking about all afternoon. And now that he had Kylie's full attention, he really wanted her opinion.

Kylie blinked. "Wow. That came out of nowhere."

Johnny shrugged. "I worry about a lot of things. I'm starting to wonder if it's all necessary. I mean, when I was in high school, I was worrying about going to college. Now that I'm going to college, all I can worry about is winning the tournament so I have more money for college. What happens if I win the tournament? What will the new obsession be?"

"I don't get it. What does all that have to do with being too grown-up?"

"Danny and Kevin go out every other night to see bands, to ride the coasters, to shoot darts for stuffed animals for their girlfriends," Johnny replied. "I haven't been to that stupid pier for anything. I'm just not interested."

"Being mature isn't a crime, Johnny," Kylie said. "If you've outgrown that kind of stuff, so be it. Move on and concentrate on what does interest you."

"That's just it," Johnny said. "I've never been interested in that kind of stuff. It's always been that way with me. I've always been the one worrying about the future, working for tomorrow, and getting stressed out when anything jeopardizes it. I mean, sometimes I feel like I'm thirty. Everything I do—all my conscious and unconscious acts—are intended for the future. I save all my money. I don't gamble, smoke, or drink. I don't stay out late. I was never comfortable until I had a steady girlfriend, someone who I knew would be there for me. It's like I'm sitting over a chessboard representing my life. I move pieces into position, syncing them perfectly for an attack that will never come."

Johnny noticed Kylie watching him as he spoke. Her eyes never left his face. She was taking him all in, not just his words, but his expressions, his movements. Everything.

Strange having someone actually listen to your problems, isn't it? he thought.

Kylie sat back, regarding him solemnly. "I think you're saying that everything you have is for a reason—to get to something, to ease something, whatever. So you're stuck with stuff you don't really want since it's all to make something else better.

Something that doesn't really exist." She laughed. "Do I even know what I just said?"

Johnny smiled. "You're close, that's for sure." He sighed, toying with a straw. "All I know is that this summer should be the one with the least amount of uncertainty. But here I am spilling my guts about how nothing seems to fit." He counted off on his fingers. "I'm going to college, check. I've got some seed money in all the right mutual funds, check. I'm set to kick butt in the tournament, check. I'm set to cash that championship check, check."

"And you've got a girlfriend you love with great long-term prospects in Jane," Kylie finished. "I'm mentioning her in the context of what you're saying, so it's okay."

Johnny glanced up at her. She was right to add Jane to the mix. Because the long-time girlfriend was a big part of his whole issue. "Check."

"It's okay to be you, Johnny. I happen to think you're a great guy." Kylie smiled at him. "Maybe you're just doing some changing this summer. Seeing things in a new way. Or seeing how things could be done a different way and still work for you."

He nodded. "I always thought my way *was* the right way. That my knucklehead brothers with their 'whatever' attitudes would get nowhere. But you know what? They're having a blast."

The waiter delivered four steaming slices of pizza and their sodas. Johnny's stomach grumbled. He was starving. Getting all that off his chest had worked up his appetite—and lightened his mood considerably.

They tore into the pizza and slurped their sodas, talking about different things but nothing with any more philosophical gravity than chewing gum. Soon they were laughing at each other again. And for a little while Johnny felt natural again. Felt happy again. The weight of the world was set aside, at least for now. They were just Johnny and Kylie. Work partners. Friends. It seemed so easy.

The sun was sinking into the sea by the time they left the pizza joint. They strolled down the boardwalk toward his apartment, their knapsacks slung over their shoulders, their pace lazy. The conversation turned toward work.

"I really like the hotel beach," Kylie commented. "I wish I could've been there all summer."

"It would've made the place nicer, that's for sure," Johnny said, trying not to imagine where their friendship would be if that had actually happened. Three months next to Kylie? "But rich people can be nasty. The cabana boys get it the worst. My brothers could tell you stories that would make your faith in humanity disappear."

"That's okay," Kylie replied. "Because you would have been there to cheer me up."

"Scary thought," Johnny replied, feeling a sudden tightness in his throat.

"Why's that?"

He chuckled coolly. "Ask my brothers. I'm usually the person making everyone miserable, not cheering them up."

Kylie reached out and touched his arm. "Don't

sell yourself short, Johnny. You've made me feel better every day we've worked together. You're a rock. I thought this summer would be a total washout. But since I've met you, I honestly look forward to coming to work. I've definitely forgotten all about Paul and his Fizz Cola girl, that's for sure."

A wave of adrenaline coursed through him. Excitement. Fear. All the things he'd been feeling all night and all day but couldn't (wouldn't) acknowledge.

She's not helping things, is she? he thought.

"That's about the nicest thing anyone's said to me." He reached out and squeezed her hand.

She squeezed back.

Johnny released her hand. He would have done anything to prolong the moment, but the dark waters of his conversation with Jane boiled inside. *I love you. . . . I'd never do anything to hurt you. . . .*

Soon his apartment building was looming over them. The sun had dipped below the waves, leaving a glowing crimson sky behind. The lamps above the boardwalk winked to life above them.

"This is you?" Kylie asked.

Johnny nodded. "You need a lift home?"

Kylie shook her head. "The walk will do me some good."

"Okay."

They stood staring at each other for a moment. Johnny felt the seconds tick away. Then, as he gazed into her beautiful eyes, at her perfect face, Johnny came to a wild and surprising conclusion. He was amazed he hadn't made the connection before.

He had just been on a really great date.

Uh-oh.

"Thanks for letting me bend your ear," he said, wondering how lame he sounded.

"Anytime, Johnny," Kylie replied, smiling.

"I wanted to hold your hand back there," he said, his voice cracking. He cleared his throat. "I wanted to more than anything else in the world—"

Kylie stepped closer to him. Closer. She slipped her arms around his neck.

And hugged him.

Every denial washed away within him as he felt her pressed against him. Every feeling he'd refused to feel, he now felt without shame. He wanted to be closer to her; he was. He wanted to know what it would be like to hold her in his arms; he now did. Everything about her was perfect. The curve of her back. The feel of her bathing suit beneath her T-shirt. The warm pressure of her body against his.

He looked into her eyes, seeing everything he was feeling reflected back at him. It would be so easy to kiss her. So easy.

But suddenly something was wrong. Kylie jumped out of their embrace, her eyes focused over his shoulder, above his head.

"Oh no," Kylie whispered.

Johnny turned around and looked up.

Standing on the balcony of his apartment, staring down at him, was Jane.

Nine

JOHNNY IMMEDIATELY JUMPED back too. He looked up at Jane to make sure she wasn't a hallucination. Johnny couldn't make out the details of her face from that distance and in the dark, but he knew fairly well what her expression said.

After another second Jane turned away from the railing and went inside.

Johnny whirled to Kylie. Her face registered shock, the same expression Johnny imagined was on his own face.

"This is bad," Johnny muttered, pacing back and forth.

"It was a hug, Johnny," Kylie said, sounding like she was trying to convince herself, too. "That's all. Just a hug between two coworkers saying good-bye for the day. After what we went through yesterday, it makes sense that we've grown closer. You didn't do anything wrong, okay?"

"Tell that to Jane," he said weakly, staring up at the now empty balcony.

"She saw her boyfriend hugging another girl," Kylie said. "And not just another girl—the girl she hates. Of course she's going to be upset. But you didn't do anything wrong," she repeated.

Johnny's mind raced. Thinking of things to say that would make sense to Jane. But nothing would make what Jane saw okay. Nothing. He *hadn't* been hugging just *another girl,* which would have been bad enough. He'd been holding Kylie. And Jane would never forgive him.

"I'm gonna go try to handle this," he told her. "I'll, um, see you tomorrow."

Kylie looked like she'd burst into tears at any minute. "I feel awful, Johnny. This is all my fault."

He gazed into her eyes, which were so full of sadness and worry and something else he couldn't quite define. "There were two of us in that embrace, Ky."

He turned to head into the building. "I don't know what I'm going to say to Jane, but I'll figure something out on my way up, I hope."

Kylie was following him. "And I'm going to help you."

"What?"

"Johnny, there's no way anything you say will make things all right," she insisted. "In her eyes, she caught you hugging me, plain and simple. What excuse could you give to convince her it was no big deal, just two good friends saying good-bye?"

"Well, what can *you* say?" he asked, running a

hand through his hair. "Jane isn't exactly your biggest fan."

"I know. That's why it's me she's gotta hear it from."

The three-flight walk was like a death march to the gallows.

Now you're being melodramatic. You screwed up. Bad. You went too far, and you got caught—blown out of the water. Now you have to face Jane. You have to go up there and explain something. Or not. It's up to you. Either way, you have to face her.

Johnny took a deep breath and slid his key into the lock.

All the lights were on. Kevin and Penny were nowhere to be seen. Danny and Raven, however, sat on the sofa, looking more uncomfortable than a couple of punk rockers waiting to see the principal. Sitting up straight. Hands folded in laps. Eyes front.

Jane leaned against the back of the recliner. Under the circumstances Johnny thought she looked great (except for the scowl). Her brown hair fell to her shoulders, and her cheeks were flushed, but that could have been from the summer sun. She wore a plain white T-shirt, khaki shorts, and sandals. Her legs were long and tan, almost glowing in the yellow apartment light. Her arms were folded across her chest. Johnny could see the tan line beneath the watch that he bought her last Christmas.

Yeah, that was Jane. How many times had he brushed that hair away from those smooth cheeks?

How many times had he kissed those full lips good night? Looked into those brown eyes? Dreamed of her slim frame? He'd always thought she was pretty hot, even though some might call her bookish. She wore glasses to read, but now those baby browns were lasered in on Johnny, as dark as coffee and running just as hot.

He slowly pulled his keys from the lock and flipped them into his palm. "Hi, Jane," he said softly.

Jane straightened to her full height, which still only brought her eye level to his chin. How many times had they slow danced, with her head nestled in the crook of his neck?

Stop with the flashbacks! What are you trying to do, have the life of the relationship flash before your eyes before it dies?

Where did that thought come from? he wondered. Did he want his relationship with Jane to die?

"I came early," Jane explained, her voice quiet and even. But Johnny could tell by her expression that she was waiting to explode. "Your voice sounded funny on the phone. I thought maybe the rescue was a lot for you to handle. I thought maybe I could help."

The rescue. She might be talking about Harold O'Hearn, but he knew she really meant the rescue of her boyfriend. Saving Johnny from Kylie's clutches. The very clutches she'd just seen him in.

Jane slowly closed the distance between them. "I guess I was wrong."

"Jane, I—"

Johnny never got a chance to finish the sentence. Jane's hand whipped out and smacked him across the cheek. He recoiled from the blow, the right side of his face suddenly numb, then scorching hot. Johnny caught a glimpse of Danny and Raven, their eyes as big as baseballs.

"How could you?" Jane said, her voice still restrained. But tears had formed, waiting to drop. "How? How could you touch her? After everything I told you about how I feel about her? How could you touch that . . ."

Kylie entered behind Johnny. He felt her slip inside next to him. He didn't dare look at her, however. His cheek still rang like a fire bell.

Jane's eyes leveled on Kylie as if she was the devil herself. And maybe she was to Jane.

"Say it, Jane," Kylie whispered, her voice full of emotion. "What were you going to call me?"

Jane's lips quivered. "How dare you come here."

"Did it rhyme with *witch,* Jane?" Kylie asked.

Jane laughed angrily. "Look at you, Kylie. After all this time you finally evened the score. Well, how does it feel? You sure got me. You sure yanked the carpet right out from under me from two hundred miles away."

Kylie's eyes narrowed. "Wait a minute. You think I did this because of what happened in the middle school?" Kylie glanced at Johnny, her eyes full of disbelief, but also as if to say, *Didn't I tell you she would never let this go?* "Jane, whatever you're

113

thinking, it's not true. I swear. This has nothing to do with the seventh grade."

"Save it, Kylie," Jane shot back. "Any more lies tonight and I think I'll puke."

Suddenly Danny was between them, leading Raven by the hand toward the front door. "Ahem. Excuse me. As much as we'd love to stay and hear all the lies from all you guys, we really have to go."

If Danny wanted an answer, he certainly didn't wait for it. He and Raven slipped through the war zone and pulled the apartment door shut behind them.

Nice getaway, Johnny thought grimly. *Should've grabbed Raven's hand and gone along.*

"Jane, you have it all wrong," Johnny said desperately. He felt a little more freedom to speak now that Danny and Raven had left. "This isn't some plot Kylie cooked up to get back at you."

Jane huffed contemptuously. "And I guess you believe that because she told you? She's a worthless liar, Johnny." Jane leveled the death stare on Kylie once again. "Always was, always will be."

Kylie stepped forward, her voice sincere. "You're wrong, Jane. We're different people now. I know how it feels to be betrayed. I know how it feels to have someone you love cheat on you. It happened to me this summer, only a few weeks ago. I wouldn't inflict that pain on anyone."

"But you just did!" Jane snarled, her voice cracking. A tear shot down her cheek.

"It's not . . ." Kylie's voice trailed off. "It was

just a hug . . . ," she added lamely, but she knew Jane had her on that one.

"Jane, you have to forget about seventh grade," Johnny said. "What happened down on that boardwalk has nothing to do with that. I mean, that fight was so long ago."

"Not so long ago, Johnny," Jane replied hatefully. "About three minutes ago by my count. Because I just caught her with her arms around my boyfriend. You, Johnny." Another tear fell, with more to come. Her expression melted into despair. "You. Johnny Ford. I never would've believed that you of all people would cheat on me. And with *her*? It's like it's not even real."

With that, Jane broke down into sobs. Johnny wanted to reach out and comfort her, wrap her in his arms and make it all go away. But he couldn't. He figured it would just make things worse. He turned to Kylie.

"Maybe you should go," he whispered, eyes desperate. "I need to talk to Jane. And you're just . . ."

He didn't want to say *making things worse,* but that's exactly what he meant. Instead of being able to help matters, Kylie had been stuck in the position of defending herself against Jane's attack. He worried that Kylie would be upset, but she only took a deep breath, wiped her eyes, and nodded.

"I'm sorry, Jane," she whispered.

As she turned to the door, she gave him a look that said, *I wish you could come with me.* A look that told him that Kylie stood by him. That Jane didn't scare her. That she would take Johnny in an instant if Jane decided to break up with him. It was a strange feeling. Disconcerting.

Could Kylie have been plotting this all along as one last junior-high hurrah against Jane?

No, he thought. No way. Not the girl he'd come to know.

Come to like very, very much.

The door clicked shut behind her, and it was just the two of them. Under normal circumstances Johnny would have welcomed time alone with Jane. He hadn't seen her for forever. But now . . . now that was utterly destroyed.

Jane whirled away from him and crossed into the living room. She stared through the sliding-glass door at the pitch-black ocean beyond.

He stared at her back. More visions of their past rose in his mind. The first time they met. Dinner at her parents' house. The tenth-grade semiformal. The junior-class trip. The senior prom.

He wanted to wrap his arms around her, make all her pain go away.

This was the girl he'd loved for three years, the girl he'd done everything with. He always thought "Class Couple" was kind of a joke, but now he realized what it really meant. Everyone else saw them as inseparable. Together forever, la-da-da-da, just as Kylie had described. Johnny never thought of it that way before. Was he really prepared to leave her? Was he prepared to inflict the ultimate hurt on her for Kylie? Granted, his attraction to Kylie went deeper than just skin, but still . . . he had to make a choice. And Jane was that choice. He knew her. He loved her still. Jane was the right thing to do.

That's the bottom line, isn't it?

Johnny stepped forward. "Jane, I just want to say that—"

"That you never meant for this to happen, right?" Jane said, refusing to face him. "That Kylie doesn't mean anything to you, right? That it was just a stupid hug, it meant nothing, it's not like you kissed her, right?"

Johnny sighed. "Right."

"If Kylie hadn't spotted me standing up here, Johnny, you would have kissed her. You would have been making out with her down there. I know it. And you know it. And that witch knows it. Once again she got me. And got me good."

She was right, he realized. Not about Kylie. But about him. He would have kissed her. He wouldn't have been able to resist. And perhaps then he would have finally surrendered to his feelings. But Kylie *had* spotted Jane. And they *had* broken apart. And they *hadn't* kissed.

"And if I wasn't here, you'd still be kissing her," Jane continued. "Right now. You might even be doing more than kissing. Because I would've been safely tucked away at Camp North Star, four hours away in the woods. Blissfully unaware of my boyfriend's arms holding someone else close." She turned to glare at him. "Look me in the eye and tell me I'm wrong."

"I won't do that." Johnny shook his head. He wouldn't lie to her. Jane deserved better than that. And so did Kylie.

"Wow, a breakthrough," Jane said in mock amazement. "God, Johnny, you're so pathetic. You can't even see that you're being used by her to get to me. One little flip of her blond ponytail, a wiggle of her butt, and a flash of blue bathing suit, and you're hooked. I thought you were deeper than that."

A twinge of anger hit Johnny. "Hold on, Jane. I'll be the first to admit I was out of line. But you're making it out to be some kind of skin thing. After the rescue, Kylie and I got carried away. It was intense. It was emotional. And we're the only ones who could understand how we felt saving a life. So we talked about it. We didn't have anyone else to talk to, so we went to each other. And I let her get closer than I should have."

"Brilliant psychological explanation, Dr. Ford," Jane said sarcastically. "Just like in the movies, right? The guy and the gal in the intense, life-threatening situation turn to each other's lips for support."

Johnny shook his head, disgusted. "It's not that simple," he said, slumping on the arm of the recliner.

Jane looked him in the eye. "So you have feelings for her?"

Uh-oh. Watch it, Johnny.

"Feelings is too general a term," Johnny said. If you're asking if I have a connection with her, yes."

"Do you want to be with her or me, Johnny?" Jane asked. "You can't have it both ways."

He stared down at the floor, his mind completely shot. He had no idea how he felt all of a sudden. About anything. "I love you, Jane. I always have and—"

"I didn't ask you if you loved me. I asked you who you want."

Johnny sighed. "I'm sorry, Jane. I'm so sorry this happened."

Jane approached him. She ran a finger along his jaw, lifting his chin so she could look him right in the eye. It was the first tender gesture she'd shown him, and it gave him hope. Johnny could see what were once warm brown eyes, eyes so inviting that he could melt into them. She was so close now. So close. Would they ever be this close again?

"You're sorry?" she whispered.

He nodded, feeling the gentle touch of her hand under his chin.

"Maybe you are truly sorry, Johnny," she said, a delicate smile curling her lips. Another tear rolled down her face. "But you're not sorry for what you did. You're sorry for getting caught. You're sorry for hurting me. And there's a monumental difference."

She pushed his face away.

"Good-bye, Johnny," she said, her voice suddenly strong. "We're through."

"Jane, I—"

He didn't even know what he was going to say. Jane was breaking up with him? He couldn't even fathom it. He'd forgotten a world that didn't have him and Jane as a couple in it.

"Kylie can have you," she snapped. "Make sure she knows I broke up with you and not the other way around."

"Jane, please, listen to me," he began.

"No, you listen, Johnny," Jane said, tears pooling in her eyes. "I hate you. I hate you so much!"

And then she ran for the door, the tears falling.

Ten

"No." JOHNNY LEAPED to his feet. He grabbed Jane's shoulder and turned her toward him. "You can't leave, Jane."

"Let go of me, Johnny," she warned, eyes livid.

Johnny lifted his hand from her shoulder. But his voice was no less urgent. "We're not through, Jane. Not by a long shot. Everyone makes mistakes. I made a big one tonight. But I believe you've been making one since the seventh grade. Kylie's not like you say she is. And no matter what, you've let that anger burn you up inside for way too long."

"What do you know about it?" Jane spat.

"Kylie told me everything," Johnny replied. "Sit down, and I'll tell you everything she told me."

She narrowed her eyes but slowly moved over to the sofa. When she dropped down, a deep breath escaping her, he knew she'd at least hear him out.

He told Jane exactly what Kylie told him. He

could tell by the hardening of her expression that everything he knew was true.

"Okay, so you know," Jane challenged. "But what does that have to do with us?"

"Everything," Johnny replied. "Because I think you were lying too. You didn't come down here because you were worried about me. You came down here because ever since Kylie and I started working together, you couldn't stand *not* being here. You had to see her for yourself. You had to personally monitor her behavior while we worked together."

Jane sighed. "Okay, okay, maybe you're right, Johnny. But so what? I mean, every suspicion I had was right! She *was* trying to steal you!"

"She wasn't trying to steal me!" Johnny exclaimed. "What happened between us just happened. There's no master plan at work here. There's no conspiracy. We had a connection, we made the mistake of acting on it, and that's it. It was a hug, Jane. A hug between two people who've become good friends."

Jane got right in his face. "How am I supposed to believe that? After all I saw tonight? Give me one good reason why I should think that you and Kylie won't be sneaking hugs tomorrow at work. After all, what could possibly bring you closer than this? Your girlfriend catches the two of you hugging at night. You and Kylie will have hours of great conversation out of this one."

Johnny counted off on his fingers. "One, because you caught me red-handed and I don't have any reason to lie to you anymore. You know now: Kylie and I are more than just partners. We're good friends. And two, because if you let me, I'll prove it to you."

Jane didn't answer right away. She regarded Johnny suspiciously. Johnny had to admit that he didn't like it. He was so used to Jane gazing into his eyes for peace, not for war. "How will you prove it?" she finally asked.

"Stay," he said simply.

"Oh, come on, Johnny." She moaned.

"No, I'm serious," he pleaded. "Stay. It's only three days until the tournament. I get off work every day at four. We'll have lots of time to spend together. And you can come to the hotel beach during the day. Then you can see firsthand what I'm talking about. If I'm right, then it's all business between me and Kylie from now on. But if you're right, she can't possibly pull off some diabolical plan while you're sitting on the beach, right?"

Jane folded her arms, eyeing Johnny skeptically. "I don't know."

"I'll do anything to make it right, Jane," Johnny said. "Anything."

He would, he realized. Because Jane was his girlfriend. Jane was his history. Jane was the girl he owed so much to. His allegiance, his loyalty. His respect.

How he dared to disrespect her the way he had was repugnant.

Johnny Ford didn't do that. No matter what, he'd never become that kind of person. And now he had to make it up to Jane. And make it up to her good.

So what happens to Kylie? a little voice inside his head piped up. *What becomes of her? Do you just forget*

*she exists? Let her deal with this herself? Act all busi-
nesslike at work for the rest of the summer?*

Kylie knew you had a girlfriend, he reminded himself.
She knew someone else had your heart. She took a risk.

And she got burned, big time.

Like that's all her fault? he asked himself. *You were
there. You smiled at her, you laughed with her, you comforted her, you told her your deepest thoughts and worries.
You, you, you.*

Could he just let it go? Let Kylie go?

Tears fell down Jane's cheeks, and she cried.
Cried on his sofa, cried because of him. He'd
never made Jane cry. He'd upset her, he'd annoyed
her, he'd angered her. But he'd never hurt her so
badly that she cried.

Suddenly it was too much. His heart broke for
her, ached for her.

"Please, Jane," he said, rushing to sit next to her.
"Please. Now that you're here, now that I see you,
everything's suddenly very real for me. I could
never be without you, Jane. Never. I love you."

She said nothing. She had stopped crying,
though. She stared at her lap as she wiped her cheeks.

"You're choosing me," she said simply. A state-
ment, not a question.

"Of course I'm choosing you, Jane," he said.
"You're my girlfriend, I love you."

She wiped the last of her tears away and let out a
massive sigh. Her eyes were still full of mistrust.
"Okay, Johnny. I'll stay."

*   *   *

Johnny set up Jane in Danny's bedroom. He threw Danny's ample laundry into the dingy little closet and called the joint clean. Jane brought her bag into the room and asked for some privacy. Johnny obliged. She said she was exhausted, and maybe she was. But Johnny saw something else there. Anger. Sadness. The sickening feeling that she had to deal with this problem hundreds of miles from home, all by herself in a disaster area of an apartment with a cheating boyfriend and two brothers who'd never spent much time with her before. She crashed at ten and didn't come out again.

As the night wore on, Kevin and Danny eventually returned from their various adventures. Danny had filled Kevin in on the night's main event, and even though he was noticeably miffed about losing his bedroom, Danny bunked down with Johnny in the living room without much complaint.

Johnny let Danny have the couch while he splayed out in the recliner, remote in hand, the only light coming from the TV tuned to a late night replay of the Dodgers game.

It was well past two when Danny finally said, "Can you can it for the night, bro?"

"No," Johnny replied.

Danny rolled over and glared at him. "What's with you anyway?"

"What do you think?" Johnny asked.

"I hope one stupid hug from Kylie was worth it, bro. Because in case you're keeping score, you just created a major distraction to this volleyball team only three days from the tournament."

"Give it a rest, Dan," Johnny grunted.

"Like hell," Danny shot back. "If Kevin or I had set off this bomb so close to the opening serve, you'd be pinning us up against the nearest wall with accusations. It pisses me off, dude."

Johnny waved him off. "So be pissed. You don't know what you're talking about. You don't know what I'm feeling."

"Oh yes, I forgot about the impenetrable Johnny Ford psyche. It's like some New York nightclub where only the chosen few are allowed past the velvet ropes. If you aren't blond, with a Reese Witherspoon body, forget it."

"Lay off Kylie," Johnny said. "This isn't her fault."

"That's right," Danny replied. "It's your fault from day one. And now it's pretty simple. You pick Kylie, or you pick Jane. This bringing both to the beach like a couple of Frisbees is the worst idea I ever heard."

A thump came from back in the bedrooms. Johnny gazed down the hallway, but all was dark. The thump didn't repeat.

"What choice do I have?" he asked, his voice hushed. "If Jane walks out of here, I lose her forever. I'm not ready for that. This is the only way I can convince her that I want us to continue. And that Kylie isn't working some devious conspiracy to tip the scales from seventh grade."

"What do you even care?" Danny asked. "I mean, about the Jane-slash-Kylie trouble. That doesn't even concern you."

"It does," Johnny told him. "It concerns me a lot. Because my girlfriend is consumed by it. Even when Kylie wasn't a blip on her radar screen the past three years, she was thinking about it. About the time she'd been miserable because of Kylie. That's a part of Jane—a part of her that I as her boyfriend need to respect."

Danny sighed. "Hey, big bro." His voice was serious. "What now?"

"I'm only going to say this once 'cause I know you'll remember it, and it comes from Kevin too. Keep your head in the game. Danny and I stepped in our piles already, but we straightened ourselves out for this tournament. Don't blow it now. You said yourself that this summer is about the tournament. Nothing else matters."

Johnny turned to Danny. "Nothing else matters? I've been in love with Jane for three years. That matters, Dan."

"Jane shouldn't even be here, Johnny. You should've just let her go. Let things cool off. We win the tournament so you can pay for college, then you fix things with Jane. But this stupid plan of yours? Talk about distractions."

Johnny cracked his knuckles, mindlessly watching Gary Sheffield hit a home run. "I can handle it."

"Can you?" Danny asked. "I wonder, bro. I really wonder. And you want my opinion?"

Johnny sighed. "Go ahead."

"I don't think you've been in love with Jane for three years," Danny whispered.

"Huh?" Johnny said. "What are you talking about? Of course I have."

"No, John. You've been her *boyfriend* for three years. Her status quo boyfriend. Maybe you were in love with her when you first met her, or maybe you just found someone who lived and breathed life the same way you did. But there's a big difference between being in love and being comfortable. Trust me, I know. I have a girlfriend with pink hair and a navel ring."

Johnny turned to face Danny, but it was too dark to see his face. He settled back in the recliner. "I'm tired," he said, clicking off the television.

"So I'm right," Danny whispered.

"I never said that," Johnny muttered, shifting in the chair.

"You didn't have to, big bro. You never walk away from an argument unless you know you're shot."

Johnny blinked. When had his knucklehead brothers gotten to know him so well? And when had they gotten so smart?

Danny eventually dozed off, snoring lightly. Johnny turned on the television again, lowering the volume so he could hardly hear it. The Dodgers won. A *Seinfeld* rerun came on after that. Johnny set down the remote and got up to get a glass of water.

He tiptoed into the dark kitchen and searched the cabinets for a clean glass. He wished he had the energy to wash the mound of dishes in the sink; he hated the idea of Jane waking up to dirty dishes and a messy apartment.

He heard a door clicking and peered down the hallway. Jane had just come out of the bathroom. She'd been so quiet that he never heard her.

She was frozen in the dim lights coming through the windows, a combination of long-distance street-lamps and starlight that illuminated her silhouette just enough so he could see her face. She stared right at him. She wore a long T-shirt and nothing else.

She looks so vulnerable. Danny was wrong. Johnny did love her.

He did.

How could he ever think of cheating on that girl? How could he ever have let her slip from his mind enough to let another girl take her place—even if it was for a split second?

Look at her. She used to be yours. Will she ever be again?

They stared at each other for what seemed like a light-year. There was no sound except for the gentle roar of the surf out the window. Danny's heavy breathing. Nothing else.

Johnny wondered what she was thinking. Was she hating him right now, at that moment? Or was she seeing the guy she loved in his most basic state, stripped to boxer shorts, unable to sleep, and so, so sorry?

So this is us. The couple on the rocks. Eyeing each other with both pure distrust and utter need.

Before Johnny could say anything, Jane turned away, shut the bedroom door, and locked it tight.

Eleven

JOHNNY ARRIVED AT work early the next morning to discover that the Surf City 3-on-3 Beach Volleyball Tournament had come to town. The courts, nets, and grandstands were being assembled on the hotel beach. Trucks parked on the sand. Workers hauled long chunks of steel, putting it all together with the whir and *clack-clack* of hydraulic air guns.

This is it, he thought. *This is where it will all finally happen.*

He felt a surge of adrenaline. He wanted to grab a volleyball and play right then and there. That was a good sign. The desire was still there. The girls hadn't driven it from him completely.

Johnny needed any edge he could get. For he knew that Danny was right about one thing. Kylie and Jane would be a monumental distraction—if he let them. All he had to do was keep his mind on

131

the game, his eye on the prize. Yeah, it was all coming together now.

Jane had still been sleeping by the time Johnny and his brothers left for work. Danny and Kevin had taken one look at Johnny's expression, and they'd shut up the whole ride to the hotel. They knew he wouldn't let them down at the tourney.

Johnny spotted Kylie walking toward him. She was dressed for work as always in her blue one piece, shades on, hair back. Instantly Johnny was reminded of just how hard it was going to be to concentrate. On volleyball. On repairing his relationship with Jane. On anything. Her sunglasses helped. They kept her eyes hidden.

He didn't know what he'd do if had the opportunity to look into those eyes.

For now, it was time for work. Johnny climbed into the chair. Kylie spent some time at the shed, then joined him. He put out his hand to help her up, which she took.

"Thanks," she said softly. "How, um . . . how did it go last night?"

"I'm not sure we should talk about that," he said, hating himself. It was a little late to stop talking about Jane behind her back.

"Oh."

"Yeah."

Kylie spoke cautiously. "So . . . what does that mean?"

"It means that I managed to salvage something out of our relationship," Johnny replied. Kylie flipped her sunglasses atop her head. Damn. He watched her expression as he added, "Jane decided to stay."

Kylie's face didn't change, which relieved Johnny. Sort of. He didn't know what he'd expected. He only knew that he didn't want to be responsible for hurting this girl.

He wasn't responsible, was he? Hadn't he worked that out last night? She'd known Johnny was spoken for. She'd known. And she'd taken the risk. That was Kylie, right? Taking risks? That was what he admired about her. That was why he—

Johnny froze, unwilling to finish the thought. Unwilling to go there, to even think about it.

"That's good, right?" Kylie asked, turning those blue-green eyes on him.

Johnny nodded. "Well, nothing's fixed yet. All we've done is decide to try and fix it. I owe her that, Kylie."

"Owe her?" Kylie asked.

"Yeah, owe her. She's my girlfriend. She saw me embracing another girl. You, of all people. Yeah, I owe her."

"Me, of all people," Kylie repeated dully.

"Kylie . . . ," he began, unsure what to say. He knew what he needed to do now. He needed to make things right with Jane. He needed to focus on the tourney. On winning. And he needed to ignore his attraction to Kylie. His feelings for her. He could do that. Just push it away. Push it far away. He could do that. He'd been doing that for years.

"So this is what you want, Johnny?" she asked. "You're sure?"

Johnny wasn't expecting that question. More to the point, he wasn't prepared to answer it. What he wanted and what he should do were two different things. "Yeah," he finally said, lying and not liking it. "It's the right thing."

He noticed a look of pain pass over Kylie's face. A split second, then it was gone. It wasn't the look of a girl whose massive plan had just been thwarted. It was the look of a girl who'd just been stung by heartbreaking news.

You're not responsible, he reminded himself. *You're not.*

So why did he feel so guilty?

And why did he feel as heartbroken as she looked?

"I think that's great, Johnny," Kylie finally replied. The hurt was all gone, at least on the surface. "If that's what you want to do."

Did Kylie really mean it? Or was she smoothing over the cracks in her facade?

"Look, Kylie, I want you to know that—"

"So are you getting psyched for the tournament?" she interrupted. "Those grandstands are huge. I didn't think they were expecting so many people."

She was letting him off the hook, he realized. Changing the subject. She knew that was what he wanted, what he needed, and she was giving it to him. He sent her a silent thank-you. He wasn't sure if she heard it, but he had a feeling she did.

"Um, yeah, I guess they are," Johnny answered,

glancing at the construction of the courts. "Before you know it, we'll be spiking our way to immortality. On this beach anyway."

Kylie smiled. Then she leaned back and scanned the water.

So that's it? he wondered. He'd told her what the situation was. They'd briefly talked about the tournament, and now they were supposed to act like nothing was wrong.

A few hours passed. The surf grew rougher. Around noon a riptide warning came over the radio. Johnny and Kylie brought in the flags and whistled some swimmers closer to shore. The waves pounded the water, chasing many of the bathers back to the pool. The beach was lame anyway since the emerging volleyball court and grandstand took up so much room. But enough swimmers stayed in the water for Johnny and Kylie to remain alert.

"I'm sorry," Kylie suddenly said.

Johnny turned to face her, his heart squeezing.

"I'm sorry," she repeated, not taking her eyes from the ocean. "For creating so many problems. It's all my fault."

It is her fault—not the problems. Her pain. I'm not responsible. She took the risk. She knew I had a girlfriend. And she knew Jane was coming down here. It is her fault. I'm not responsible.

How many times was he going to keep repeating that? Johnny wondered. Until he believed it?

"You didn't do anything, Kylie. The trouble

between me and Jane isn't your fault. It's mine." That was the truth. No one had forced Johnny to spend time with Kylie outside of work. And no one had forced him to embrace her in the moonlight.

"I was there too," Kylie said evenly. "But I swear to you, Johnny, I didn't go after you to get back at Jane. I went after you because . . . I'm crazy about you. I think you know that, though. You're everything I've ever wanted in a boyfriend. After Paul hurt me, I didn't think I'd be interested in anyone for a long time. But you've seen me at my best and at my worst. And you never judge. You're just you. I wish I could've known you a long time ago."

Kylie paused, then let out a deep, exhausted sigh. "But I'm going to bow out gracefully. I'm not gonna give you a hard time or make a scene or tell you I know you have feelings for me too. You've made a decision. And I'll respect that. But I won't sit here and let you go without at least telling you how I feel."

Johnny swallowed and stared down at his feet. There was so much he wanted to say to her. So much he wanted to explain. He wanted to tell her how much she had come to mean to him too. That their brief time together had stirred feelings to the surface that he'd been too afraid to explore.

No. Not afraid. Johnny Ford wasn't afraid of anything. He was simply committed to another girl. And he honored his commitments. There was no choice here to make. Jane was his girlfriend, period.

"Thank you, Kylie," he whispered.

"For what?"

"For everything you just said," he answered softly. "And for everything in general."

They didn't speak for a while after that.

Jane did indeed come to the hotel beach. Not long after lunch she stopped about a dozen yards to the left of the chair and spread out a blanket. Johnny spotted her and waved. She waved back but didn't smile.

"Watch the chair for me?" Johnny asked Kylie.

"Sure," she said, without expression.

Johnny jumped down and went to greet Jane. She pulled off a T-shirt and shorts to reveal a pink bikini. Johnny was surprised to see how tan she was. Camp North Star must have given her a lot of time to sunbathe.

"Hi," he greeted.

Jane nodded, busily setting up shop. She'd brought suntan lotion, a magazine, a novel, and a big bottle of spring water. She squirted lotion on her legs and began rubbing it in.

"You need some help?" Johnny asked, trying not to sound too hopeful.

"Nope," Jane replied curtly. "I've got it all under control. Besides, you're on duty, right?"

"Yeah."

"Then you'd better get back to your perch," Jane said, gesturing at the chair. Kylie gazed back at them briefly, then returned her attention to the water. "Looks like she's getting lonely."

A particularly loud wave slammed the beach. Johnny sighed. So this was how it was going to be.

"If you need anything, just holler," he offered. "Kevin or Danny can get you whatever you want, on the house."

Jane smiled, and he could tell she'd let down her guard just a drop. "Sounds good. The grounds are beautiful. The hotel is really swanky too."

"Five stars," Johnny said, turning back toward the chair.

"Hey," came Jane's voice.

Johnny turned back. "Yeah?"

"Dinner tonight?" She shaded her eyes and squinted at him.

Johnny smiled. That was the expression he'd been waiting for. The crack in the wall that allowed some of Jane's normal self to shine through. Johnny felt some of the tension leave him.

"Of course," he told her. "The best place in Surf City."

Jane smiled. That was a start, he thought. At least they were on speaking and smiling terms.

He headed back to the chair. Kylie sat up there, stiff as a surfboard. She stared at the water, her face seemingly serene, her eyes covered by sunglasses.

That must have hurt her bad, he realized, watching him run over to Jane, listening to them making plans for dinner. He wondered if Jane was secretly enjoying herself, lying there in her bikini, sunning herself while Kylie worked and knowing that she'd won. She'd ended up with the guy Kylie wanted.

Again.

As the afternoon progressed, Johnny felt utterly torn. To his left sat Jane. To his right, Kylie. And it was obvious that Jane had indeed positioned herself for maximum visibility.

Jane had a fabulous figure, and she clearly knew it. He kept turning to look at her as she slathered her body with lotion.

"Watch the water, partner," Kylie finally said.

Johnny nodded. "I am."

"What's the matter?" she asked. "Haven't you ever seen a girl put on suntan lotion before?"

She asked that in a perfectly reasonable voice, with almost a chuckle to it. But Johnny heard the hurt, and he couldn't respond. He didn't know *what* to say. Suddenly things were fine (on the surface, at least) with Jane and terrible with Kylie. He felt sandwiched between the two girls. To his left, responsibility and love. To his right, the relationship that could have been, in another place and time. And these girls hated each other.

Yet he really liked them both.

Twelve

TWO DAYS PASSED. Each day was the same. Jane on the beach, Kylie on the chair. The nights were easier. He spent his time with Jane. They roamed the boardwalk; ate, saw a movie, tossed some rings for cheesy prizes. Basically did all the things a girlfriend and boyfriend were supposed to do. It was peaceful at night. Jane loosened up without Kylie around, and Johnny's mood lightened in turn.

By Friday the grandstands and nets were up. The beach looked like a real provolleyball court. *This is it,* Johnny thought as he showed up for work on Friday. *It's really going to happen. I'm really going to be playing on that gorgeous patch of sand.*

Johnny sat in position in the lifeguard chair, Kylie next to him. She had been her casual self the past few days, trying to keep things okay between them, but they'd barely spoken.

"Help! Help me!"

Johnny flew up at the cries for help. *Not again,* he prayed silently.

Kylie scanned the water with her binoculars. "There!" she said, pointing. "Three kids, fifty yards out! How did they get so far out?"

"Tide's pulling them," Johnny said, slipping Excalibur's strap over his shoulder. "Call it in, and let's go."

Kylie barked several code words into the walkie-talkie, and they jumped off the chair and sprinted past a startled Jane for the water.

Johnny kicked through the shallows and dove head-on into a massive wave. It was like hitting a thick pane of glass. *Man, it's rough today,* he thought. *Should've been watching closer.* He came up on the other side of the wave, and the tide immediately and savagely pulled him out to sea. Kylie was several feet to his right. He could see by her expression that she felt it too.

The pair chopped their way through the swells and breakers toward the trio of kids in trouble. On every breath Johnny made sure he kept them in sight so he could swim a direct line to them.

He and Kylie reached the first kid simultaneously. "I have him," Kylie declared. "Get the others."

The boy, maybe nine or ten, was bugging out. Kylie wrapped her arms around him and used her body and life pod as a raft to prop him up in the water. "It's okay—I've got you. Just relax. You need to conserve your energy."

That's all Johnny heard. He pounded through the water toward the others, one girl and another boy. He reached the girl first and held her up as he slowly paddled to the other boy. In seconds he had them both.

"Help us!" the girl screamed. "We can't get back to shore!"

"Stay calm," he reassured them, spitting out a mouthful of water. "We've got you. Kick toward my partner, okay?"

The kids were too scared not to listen, and slowly Johnny and Kylie met up amid the waves. The shore seemed a long way off.

He caught the look in her eye.

"Can't swim it," he said.

She shook her head. "Not with three. No way."

"What do you mean, no way?" the first boy squealed. "We're going to drown out here!"

"You won't drown. I promise," Kylie said, her voice confident. But Johnny saw something else in her gaze. Fear. And this wasn't the fear they both had while rescuing Mr. O'Hearn. This was different. For now their own lives were at stake.

Johnny knew they could tread water for a little while. But the current was unpredictable and savagely strong. And his limbs were already on fire.

Minutes passed. The pain in his limbs increased. It would be bad in a few minutes. Very bad. And all he was doing was treading water. He couldn't even imagine swimming against this current.

Where's the backup? he wondered. *Where's the boat?*

Kylie's head slipped beneath the waves, and she came up coughing. Johnny linked her elbow in his and pulled her closer, but the kids on top of them were so heavy. Kylie spit out salt water and tried to breathe, but she was as out of breath as he was.

"You okay?" he asked.

She barely nodded.

The children fell strangely silent. Johnny could feel them shivering against him. Probably fear, but it could've been the water too.

"Easy, kids," he said. "Help's coming. We've got you, and we won't let you go. That's a promise, okay?"

"The shore is so far away," the girl said in a tiny voice.

Johnny looked. She was right. They had to be a good quarter mile out now and pushing to the south.

Big mistake. Looking ashore during a riptide was like looking down from a dizzying height. All you do is panic. Johnny took a deep breath and refused to cave.

What if this was it for him? For all of them? He couldn't help thinking it. He'd seen how quickly life could be snatched away with Mr. O'Hearn. They couldn't tread water forever, not in this current. He looked at Kylie. Her gaze was focused skyward on some invisible point.

"Hear that?" Kylie managed, still staring at the sky.

"No."

"I do," the second boy said. "Listen."

Suddenly Johnny heard it. An engine. An engine on a big powerboat.

"They're coming!" Kylie cried, and the children cut loose with cheers.

"Easy, easy," Johnny said. "Conserve your energy."

But relief flooded him as well. The sound was unmistakable. And within minutes the Surf City rescue boat came into view between the waves. Johnny waved Excalibur in the air and was spotted.

The boat pulled alongside them, and Beach McGriff's frizzed white hair stood out against the blue sky. "Been a busy week for you dudes," he said, smiling.

The kids were pulled on board, then Kylie, then Johnny. He collapsed in a heap on the AstroTurf floor of the boat.

After a few seconds Johnny managed to climb onto the bench at the stern. Kylie was already there, huffing.

"You okay?" she asked.

He replied by hugging her. Hard. The kind of hug between two people who had shared something so intense that only they could comfort each other. She hugged him back, holding him close.

And it was okay now. There was nothing wrong with what he was doing. He could hug Kylie; after the experience they'd just had, it was more than okay. He no longer felt guilty about her.

Because there was only one girl in his heart. He'd known it when he'd been out there in the water. The real choice had been made for him out there in the ocean, when he'd floated with his life in doubt. It was an unconscious choice, made with no more consideration than survival. And Johnny knew it had to be the right one; it was that pure an image.

For the face he saw in his mind wasn't Kylie's, but Jane's.

Jane had changed into a sundress and strappy sandals for their dinner out. Johnny put on his thin, worn jeans and a billowy white shirt that Jane liked. They strolled the boardwalk, hand in hand.

"I didn't bring this up earlier, Johnny," Jane said, pushing a strand of her silky brown hair behind her ears. "Because I know you had a really tough day. I wanted to give you time to recover before I gave you something else to deal with."

Johnny eyed her. Was she talking about the hug? Had she seen that? He doubted it. He, Kylie, and the kids had been pretty far out.

"Here we are," he said, grateful for the interruption. He held open the door to Fiesta's, the best Mexican restaurant in Surf City. The host led them through the big, bright, colorful restaurant to the back deck, where they chose a table overlooking the water. "I'm starving."

"Me too," Jane said as she sat down and placed her napkin on her lap. A waiter brought over two glasses of water, a basket of chips and salsa, and menus.

"I saw you two embrace out there," Jane said, sipping her water. "And I got it. I mean, I realized that after a situation like you'd been in, it would be natural to hug. It's like kids hugging at camp after someone hits a home run."

Sort of, Johnny thought. "Jane, I—"

"Let me finish, okay?" she said, her beautiful brown eyes trained on him. "I probably misjudged what I saw the night I arrived. I know you'd never betray me, Johnny. It's not in you. Even if you didn't love me anymore, you wouldn't betray me. You'd probably obsess over it for months and finally tell me the truth. But I should have known better than to think you'd do something so risky and stupid. Choose a maybe over a sure, three-year good thing? No way."

Johnny stared at her. He grabbed a chip and scooped up some salsa to give him time to process what she'd just said. Why had it sounded so insulting? He didn't think she'd meant it that way. But something had come across wrong.

He'd planned to tell her tonight about how her beautiful face had immediately come into his mind when he'd been out there in the water, not sure if he'd make it. How it had been Jane who'd been in his mind, his heart, when it really counted.

But suddenly he didn't want to tell her. He didn't think she'd understand, not the way Kylie would. Jane would probably simply say, *Of course you thought of me. I'm your girlfriend. You love me. Duh, Johnny.*

The waiter appeared, but Johnny's appetite had disappeared.

Thirteen

O N SATURDAY, THE day of the tournament, the Ford brothers all woke up nervous wrecks. Unusually quiet, the three of them left the apartment extra early, since they had to be on the beach by seven-thirty for sign ins. The first action started at nine. Jane was still asleep when they left. Johnny and Jane had walked along the boardwalk after they finished their meal at Fiesta's, gotten some cotton candy, talked about nothing in particular, and then had gone back to the apartment since Johnny had to wake up so early.

Why had they talked about nothing? he wondered. There was so much to say. So much they needed to discuss. So much each of them had swirling in their minds, about each other, about college, about the future. But Jane kept things surface level. *As usual*, a little voice piped up. Jane had always talked about things, not feelings. School, exams, work, parents. Even when she'd mentioned her bitter enemy, it never seemed real, as if there were real feelings attached. As if she was simply holding on to an ancient grudge for no real reason other than that it happened.

He'd tried to talk to her about yesterday's rescue, about the terror in the kids' faces. About his own fear. But maybe because Kylie had been a part of it, she didn't want to talk about it. She'd told him it was over, that there was no need to dwell on it. *What a way to end my summer as a lifeguard,* he thought now. *Three months of nothing, then two major rescues in one week.*

There was one thing he didn't mention to Jane last night: How worried he was about Kylie. It wasn't like her roommates could offer much comfort or support; she'd told him that the girls wouldn't really understand. He envisioned her walking the boardwalk, eating an ice cream cone somewhere alone, trying to comfort herself.

"Yo, Johnny," Danny called. "Let's go—we have to sign in!"

He jogged to catch up to his brothers. They beelined for the registration table and signed themselves in as the Ford team. Once the paperwork was done, the trio started tapping a ball around to warm up and burn off the excess adrenaline.

"Well, well, well," came a familiar voice. "Looks like they showed up after all."

Tanner St. John, Shooter Ridge, and Arliss Neeson appeared, bare chested, wearing two-hundred-dollar sport shades and painter hats with flip-up visors.

"Nice work on the beach yesterday, Buick," Tanner teased. "Not all shook up from your near death experience, are you?" he added in a singsong voice.

"Don't you wish," Johnny said.

"You're such a loser," Danny said to Tanner.

Johnny had to hand it to Danny. The kid was at least five inches shorter than Tanner and a lot less muscular.

Tanner grinned. "Such a charming young lad." He stepped closer to Danny, who barely made it up to Tanner's chin. "You don't have any idea what's about to happen to you, do you?"

Danny stroked his chin. "Hmmm. Maybe a volleyball game?"

"No, man," Shooter Ridge replied.

"No?" Kevin asked, mock perplexed. "Ooh, do tell us, then!"

"I'm serious, you rejects," Tanner said. "If you guys make it to the finals against us, you're going to be in a different world. A world of pain and humiliation unlike any you've ever been in before. What we're going to do, gentlemen, is scar you for life."

"I certainly hope so," Danny replied drolly.

"Anything else would be uncivilized," Kevin added.

Tanner nodded, his face stone. "Don't say you haven't been warned. Buh-bye, Chevies."

Johnny shook his head. What a moron. But Johnny knew that what Tanner had said was true. If they indeed made it to the finals against Tanner and his cronies, it would be the hardest game they would ever play.

You have to get to the finals first, bud, he reminded himself. *One game at a time.*

"Hey, big bro," Kevin said, spinning a ball on his finger. "You okay or what?"

"Why wouldn't I be?" Johnny asked, snatching the ball.

"Gee, I think her name is Jane," Danny said.

"No, actually I think her name is Kylie," Kevin added.

Johnny was thinking of a good comeback when he noticed his brothers' expressions. They were staring at the ground, staring at each other, staring at him.

They were worried. About him. About how upset he'd been the past few days and about its effect on the tourney.

"I won't let you guys down," he told them. "I give you my word."

"We know," Kevin said.

"Yeah, we know," Danny repeated.

Suddenly Johnny realized that they did know. They knew him better than he ever gave them credit for. He'd never really stopped to think about how this summer would affect their relationship as brothers. Johnny was leaving home come Labor Day. This was their stretch of time together before he took off for a new life hours away.

"I'd never let you two down," he repeated, in a voice so low, he wasn't sure they heard him.

Danny and Kevin headed for the practice area, throwing the ball at each other along the way.

Johnny smiled. He had a feeling they'd heard him loud and clear.

Kylie showed up around eight-fifteen. Johnny was relieved to see her, mostly because her presence meant that she was probably okay. She didn't wave, which didn't surprise Johnny, considering that Jane could be around. But she did smile. Johnny smiled back.

Raven, Penny, and Jane were supposed to arrive together around eight-thirty. Johnny spotted Raven walking toward him and Danny and Kevin.

"Hey, sweet thang," Danny greeted, kissing her.

"Where's Penny and Jane?" Johnny asked, emphasizing Jane. Raven suddenly looked uncomfortable. Johnny's eyes narrowed. "What?"

"Well . . . Penny will be here soon," Raven replied slowly.

Uh-oh. "And?" Johnny said expectantly.

Raven swallowed hard. "Jane asked me to give this to you."

She held out a folded sheet of paper. Johnny took it. "What's this?"

Raven shrugged, looking apologetic.

Johnny flipped open the paper, a nervous lump growing in his throat. He read:

Dear Johnny,
     I'm sorry Raven had to deliver this to you right before your match, but there was no other way. You may have figured it out by

now, but I won't be coming to the tournament. I'm leaving on the eight-forty bus to go home. We've grown so far apart. I guess I knew it even at North Star, but I didn't want to admit it. Maybe that's the real reason I came to Surf City early. Maybe I wanted to see for myself if I still felt what I used to feel for you. Seeing you with Kylie was a shock. A terrible shock. But you know that. And you know what else? I think you would've been drawn to another girl even if it wasn't Kylie sharing your lifeguard chair.

I've come to grips with the whole seventh-grade thing. Maybe it was stupid of me to carry it along all this time. But you can't understand it unless you've experienced it. Much like your rescues. I'll never understand your bond with Kylie. But one thing I do understand: When I saw the two of you go into action and work together and then embrace on the boat, I realized that you and Kylie have a true partnership. I tried to explain it away last night as a natural thing, but I spent all night tossing and turning, thinking how I really felt about it. Johnny, we'll never have that kind of partnership. And that's what I want, that kind of intimacy. We both deserve it. We've been apart all summer. We're going to different colleges. I'm not the one, Johnny. I think we both know that. It's time to say good-bye.

To old feuds. To hanging on when we
should be letting go. Yeah. It's definitely
time. Good luck in the tournament. I'll always love you and wish you the best. . . .

—Jane

"What time is it?" Johnny asked urgently.

"Eight twenty-eight," Kevin replied, glancing
down at his digital watch. "Why?"

Twelve minutes, he thought. *That's cutting it close.
But I have to try.* "I'll be back."

"What?" Danny replied, eyes wide. "What are
you talking about?"

Johnny was already walking away. "Jane's at
the bus station."

"You're crazy!" Kevin called after him. "We
have a half hour before the first match!"

"I'll be back!"

Johnny heard Danny curse and slam a ball into
the sand. He didn't care. He had to get to Jane before she got on that bus.

As he left the beach, he caught a glimpse of Kylie
on the sidelines, covering her mouth, her eyes sad.

He found her sitting on a bench at the bus station. The big clock on the wall read 8:38.

Ha! Made it.

Sweat poured down his cheeks and neck. He'd
huffed and puffed but knew in his heart that he
couldn't just let her go. He stumbled into the ter-
minal, spotted her, and ran toward her.

"Jane!"

She whirled at his voice, a look of panic on her face. She obviously thought she had made a clean getaway. "Johnny!" she cried. "What are you doing here?"

"What do you think?" he asked. "You can't leave. Not now."

She sighed. "You read the note?"

He held up the now sweat-soaked, crumpled paper. "Of course I read it. But I don't care what it says. We can work this out."

Jane smiled sadly. "Even if everything the letter says is true?"

Johnny paused. He didn't know how to answer that. Suddenly Jane's words from last night came back to him. *I should have known you'd never do something so risky and stupid. Choose a maybe over a sure thing? No way . . .*

He'd felt insulted last night, and he hadn't known why. After all, responsible, do-the-right-thing Johnny Ford *would* choose a sure thing over a maybe.

Until a girl named Kylie taught him that all you got for that was a feeling of safety. What you really wanted was still out there somewhere, waiting for you, taunting you with how much you desired it. And how much you couldn't have it because you were afraid.

Afraid. That was why Johnny had pushed Kylie away. Why he'd clung to Jane like a lifeline. *She's my girlfriend. Of course I love her.*

Suddenly Johnny wondered why he'd really

sprinted here. Had he meant to stop Jane from leaving? Or had he simply wanted to say good-bye?

No. He couldn't say good-bye. Not yet.

"Jane—"

She held up her hand. "Johnny, I spent four hours on a bus thinking about this on my way down here. I knew before I got here that we'd probably be saying good-bye. We've both been hanging on out of familiarity. But it's time to let go. I explained it all in the letter."

Johnny stared at her, stunned. He felt the lump grow in his throat. Felt the realization grow inside him that it was truly over. Three years, over.

"I can't believe this is it," he whispered. "After all this time."

Jane reached out and touched his hand. "We're both starting new lives this fall, Johnny. We're going to grow into different people. We're already different people."

Johnny nodded. He knew that everything she said was true.

"I still don't like Kylie," Jane added. "I never will. But the *hatred* is gone. I realized how stupid it was to hold on to it. It was holding me back. Maybe seeing her in action again knocked it out of me finally. I don't know. I just know I feel lighter than I have in a long time. Freer."

Johnny pushed a tendril of hair behind her ear. The loudspeaker roared to life and called Jane's bus.

"Take good care of yourself, Johnny," she said, then ran inside the depot.

Fourteen

JOHNNY ARRIVED BACK at the hotel beach at seven after nine. Volleyball games had already started on the side courts. He found his brothers waiting for him at the appointed court. Their expressions were a mixture of relief and rage.

"I don't believe you," Danny said, yanking him close to avoid making a scene. "You almost blew the whole thing."

"What happened?" Kevin asked. "Is Jane coming?"

Johnny shook his head. "No. She's gone."

"Gone?" Danny asked, sharing a look with Kevin.

Johnny nodded firmly. "Gone."

Danny sighed. "Normally I'd say, 'Sorry, dude,' but we're about to start a volleyball tournament. Are you up to this?"

"Yeah," Johnny said, lying. "Let's do it."

"Good," Kevin replied. "Because you wouldn't have a choice even if you'd said no."

The referee directed each team to their side of the court. Johnny wiped the sweat from his brow with a towel, tossing it to the sidelines. He flexed, feeling the sand between his toes. The team on the other side of the net was a sand squad from Santa Barbara, well known in their own town but nowhere else. Johnny had scouted them before and knew what they could do. If the Fords played like they were supposed to, they wouldn't have a problem.

Just before Danny's first serve, Johnny caught sight of Kylie in the crowd. Their eyes locked. Kylie. His Kylie. He felt the force of their connection slam him in the gut. He offered her a quick smile, which she returned.

She must be going nuts wondering what happened with Jane, he thought. But then the voice screamed: *Play volleyball, moron!*

He squared himself for the serve.

Just play, he told himself. *You know how, you know how. Piece of cake with icing.*

Danny served, and the tournament was on.

Ten minutes later Johnny hit the sand hard, diving to reach a ball that was unreachable. He grunted on impact, tasting sand.

"Seven—zero," came the scorekeeper's voice.

That was 7–0 in favor of the bad guys, Johnny knew. They were being shut out.

What's going on? I feel good. I'm getting good air. But I can't catch up to the ball!

He searched the stands for Kylie but couldn't find her. Then someone spun him around violently. Danny.

"What is going on with you?" he screamed. Johnny heard laughter erupt from the stands at the outburst. But Danny didn't care. "Where's your head? Is it on a bus to Spring Valley? If so, you might as well get on the bus with it, bro. Because we're not going to get past the first round. Is that what you want?"

Anger flooded Johnny. "Shut up and play, Danny," he muttered, shoving his brother aside.

Danny jumped in front of him. "No way, Johnny. This isn't just a game, man. This is our whole summer. Our whole summer! After all your preaching about staying focused, avoiding distractions, all that crap. And now you pull this. You look like you're half asleep out there! For God's sake, play!"

Johnny blinked. Took a deep breath. He knew Danny was right. Totally, utterly, absolutely right. He was here to play ball. And even though he'd told himself that over and over again, he'd still forgotten it. There was no tomorrow. If they lost this first match, they were done. Forever. Kaput. And that couldn't happen.

He had to forget everything but what he wanted at this exact moment. And that was to win this tournament. For himself. For his brothers.

Johnny sighed, closed his eyes, and felt the sweat run down his body. Felt the sand beneath his toes. The wind in his hair. It was indeed time. Everything faded from his mind. Jane. Kylie. Guilt. Heartbreak. All of it.

When he opened his eyes again, he was ready to play.

The final spike felt like a shot of adrenaline straight into his heart. The ball whizzed into the sand two feet from the nearest defender. Johnny let out a whoop as he hit the sand, high fiving Kevin and raising his arms in victory.

"That's one!" he said to his brothers.

But they had a long way to go. The Santa Barbara crew put up a good fight, but Johnny worked the net like a pro, spiking, blocking, and finally delivering twelve unanswered points. The Fords won 21–13.

The morning soon turned into afternoon. The Fords continued their hot play, going to war against three more teams and beating them all. They played like Johnny always knew they could—and would. Reading each other's tendencies. Predicting each other's moves. And using their individual talents to their greatest advantage: Danny's serves, Kevin's sets, and Johnny's spikes. They beat their opponents by an average of ten points.

When it was over, the Fords were the reigning champions of Flight B.

"Not bad, boys," Johnny said, huffing and downing a sports drink. "But we're not done yet."

"Is Flight A official yet?" Danny asked, squinting at a scoreboard.

"Don't bother," Kevin muttered. "You *know* who's going to win Flight A. It's a formality."

Five minutes later the announcement made it official: The champion of Flight A was the California University squad led by Tanner St. John.

"Big surprise," Johnny said, smiling and shaking his head. "Well . . . get ready, fellas, because the next one is for the whole ball of earwax."

The Fords were told they would have a fifteen-minute break before the final match would begin. Johnny grabbed more sports drink and slumped into a chair. He buried his face in a towel and willed the sweat to go away. It didn't work.

Someone touched his shoulder.

"Hi, partner," came Kylie's voice.

Johnny tossed the towel and looked up into her big, blue-green eyes. He grinned at her. "Hi, back."

"You played great!" she exclaimed, leaning on the railing behind him. "You guys are definitely going to win."

"I'm glad you're sure," he said, sipping his drink. "Because what you just saw was nothing. The worst is yet to come."

"You'll do great, Johnny," Kylie said. "I know it. Without a doubt. In here." She pointed at her heart and smiled.

Johnny smiled at her. He felt her faith in him.

It was as though all her belief traveled from her own heart to his.

"So, was that letter I saw Penny hand you from Jane?" Kylie asked, her expression worried. "When I didn't see her in the stands, I wondered. . . ."

Johnny stared out at the main court, where he was about to play. "Yeah. She's gone. She went home."

Kylie blinked. "She left? Before the tournament?"

He nodded. "I barely caught up to her at the bus station. It's over."

Kylie eyed him suspiciously. "So you're saying she actually broke up with you?"

"Yup," Johnny replied. "I think Jane finally realized that she was denying a lot of things. She was like me. She liked things the way they were, without change. That meant hating you and loving me. But suddenly she discovered that she really didn't do either anymore. That might have been more upsetting than seeing us in an embrace. Twice."

Kylie mulled this over. "What about you?"

Johnny glanced at her. "What about me?"

"I mean, what are you thinking?"

"About us?" he asked.

"Yeah, about us." Kylie offered a sigh of her own. "I wonder how all this will end."

Johnny turned to her. "Do you mean us . . . or the game?"

Kylie smiled at him. Just then Kevin waved and

called across the court, "Yo, Johnny! It's time. Come on."

"I have to go," Johnny said, gathering his towel and drink. This was suddenly too much for him. Jane, Kylie, the game. He had to focus. He had to.

Kylie put a hand on his shoulder and leaned in close. "Good luck," she whispered, and then she too was gone.

Fifteen

"DUDE, JUST LIKE *Gladiator*," Kevin declared, surveying the crowd in the stands.

The Fords had never played in front of a crowd, at least not one this big or this devoted to the sport. They all knew what this next match meant. And they all knew that the Ford team was a little David going up against Tanner's mighty Goliath. That comparison sat just fine with Johnny since he knew how that particular fight turned out.

Johnny picked some familiar faces out of the throng. Raven and Penny. Beach McGriff. Penny's dad, sitting with a bunch of suits, no doubt Fizz Cola reps. Mr. O'Hearn, looking hale and hearty. Doberman, Raven's brother, with his spiked hair and multiple piercings, looking as scary as always. Some of Doberman's skate-rat buds that Johnny remembered. Skunk. Motormoron. And there was Kylie, shades on, watching him intently.

He stretched and did a quick self-evaluation. Johnny felt good. Even after an entire day of volleyball, along with the stress and pressure (or stressure) that went with it, his legs felt strong. He'd been pounding the sports drinks to keep himself hydrated, forcing some on Kevin and Danny as well.

They'd come a long way and waited a long time for this moment. Now it was time to win. But Johnny had caught part of Tanner's games throughout the day. It wouldn't be easy. Just by making it to the finals, the Fords had guaranteed themselves a second-place finish, a check for a thousand dollars, and a set of Fizz Cola beach towels.

Rah, rah. A thousand clams. That's not what you came for. You came for the big prize. The ten grand. The mondo trophy. The crown of crowns. The only question is, are you man enough to take it?

Yes. The one thing Johnny Ford wasn't afraid of was winning.

The referee signaled for the players to take their positions.

Johnny took a deep breath and sneaked a quick glance at Kylie.

"Okay," he whispered. "Let's do it!"

"Joh-nny," sang Tanner from across the net. He waved like a little kid. "I see you, Joh-nny. Peekaboo, Johnny Ford! Time to die, Johnny Ford!"

"Yada, yada, yada," Johnny muttered.

"Gonna stomp your guts, Johnny boy," Shooter taunted from right across the net.

"Is someone talking?" Johnny asked Kevin.

Kevin shrugged.

Tanner's greatest advantage—his whole team's greatest advantage—was size and strength. They simply outweighed the Fords. They were older, taller, bigger, and meaner. Which could lead to intimidation. But Johnny had faith in his brothers. They'd played a lot of volleyball against some hot teams. Fear wouldn't be their problem today. It all came down to performance.

Could they do it?

Now was the time to find out. Arliss Neeson tossed the ball in the air and launched a rocket serve breaking over the net toward the sand.

"Kevin, dig!" Johnny called, but it was too late. His younger brother dove, but Arliss's serve was perfect. It hit the sand inches from Kevin's outstretched hands. Kevin cursed and spit sand. The crowd oohed and cheered the effort.

Johnny helped Kevin to his feet. "One point," Johnny said. "That's all it was."

"One–zero," the scorekeeper announced.

Several volleys later, several blocked spikes later, and several blistering Tanner returns later, the score was 9–0. The crowd was growing restless. They'd come to see a match; they were getting a massacre.

But then Tanner's team got too confident, and they turned sloppy. The Fords won the serve. Danny took full advantage. He scorched the ball across the net, the spin creating a wicked break that had the ball shooting toward Tanner but curving at the last second toward Shooter Ridge. Shooter managed to tip the ball in the air, but it was a lame bump. Arliss couldn't properly set Tanner for the spike. The ball came over soft, and Johnny deflected it back over the net into the sand.

Score: 1–9.

The crowd cheered. The game wore on. And the score crept up: 4–9 . . . 6–9 . . . 9–9 . . . and finally 11–9.

But the score slowly rose: 11–10 . . . 11–13 . . . 11–17.

Alarming numbers. And there was nothing Johnny could do to stop it. They jumped, dove, spiked, blocked. The bad guys had gotten serious and hit their groove. All the Fords could do was watch.

Danny managed to block a spike and break serve at 11–19. Now the Fords had another chance. And Johnny knew it was their last chance. If Tanner's crew won back the serve, it was all over—21 was game, set, match, and summer.

"Time to go to work," Johnny whispered, his pulse pounding in his ears. So he did. The Fords resumed their barrage of random moves, baseless strategies, and slowdown. And once again they slowly chipped away at the score.

12–19 . . . 15–19 . . . 18–19 . . .

When Johnny tied the score with a hard overhand spike into the far-left corner, he let out a whoop and pumped his fist. He was running on pure adrenaline now. He glared right at Tanner, who wore a scowl for the record books.

"Tie score," the announcer said. "Nineteen serving nineteen."

Johnny walked the ball over to Danny. His younger brother didn't have much left. He was breathing hard. "Two points, bro."

Danny nodded.

Johnny gave Kevin a thumbs-up as he returned to his position. Then he caught Tanner's eye across the net. Johnny winked at him.

"Dead meat," Tanner whispered.

All eyes turned to Danny. He wiped his brow, spun the ball in his hands, and took a deep breath. His eyes were dead on the ball, trancelike, as if willing it into the air. He tossed it, stepped up, and let out a massive grunt. The ball launched from his hands. As it passed over him, Johnny actually heard the spin of the ball burning the air like a wasp.

No one on Tanner's side could even touch it.

The crowd went nuts.

"Twenty–nineteen," said the announcer. "Game point."

Johnny let out a yell and pointed at his superserver brother. "You're the man, Dan! You're the man!"

Danny got the ball back for the next serve. Hopefully the final serve. He took a deep breath like before and prepared to launch it.

Everything seemed to slow down as Johnny realized they were on the verge of victory. But they had to win the point. They could not lose serve. They'd used every trick they could think of. It was down to who wanted it more.

"I do," Johnny whispered.

Danny hit the ball. It was a good serve but

nowhere near as nasty as the previous one. Arliss bumped it easily to Shooter. Shooter's set was perfect. Tanner went up for it, slammed it home.

Johnny was there. His hands slapped at it, catching it just enough to send it back over the net. Shooter dove for it and popped it up. Tanner was off balance but managed to tip it back over the net.

Kevin stepped into it and bumped it toward Johnny. The set was sloppy, so Danny's spike was weak. Arliss spanked the ball over to Shooter, who once again set Tanner perfectly.

But the Fords blocked it, shot after shot. The volley seemed to go on forever, neither team daring to let up an ounce. The crowd was frenzied, screaming on each hit, their voices a rising and falling wave of sound that carried Johnny forward.

Then Kevin sent a rocket spike hurtling toward the far corner of Tanner's territory. He had to dive for the save or lose the tournament. He launched himself at the ball, tipping it back toward Shooter. Johnny watched in slo-mo as Tanner's momentum carried him out-of-bounds, splayed out flat on the sand. His eyes widened, and he spun back toward the net.

Shooter managed to bump the ball for Arliss, who stepped up for the kill.

Johnny timed it.

Out of the corner of his eye he saw Tanner roll to a sitting position, still halfway out-of-bounds.

Arliss let out a roar, putting everything he had into the spike. Johnny leaped for it. He heard the smack of the ball. The finish of Arliss's grunt. Felt a spray of sweat.

He stretched to full height, lunging to get above the net.

His fingertips touched the ball . . . but to his horror, it skipped off them and over his head.

No! The spike got through!

Then Johnny felt a presence directly behind him. Heard a grunt. Kevin.

He turned in time to see his little brother tap the partially blocked spike over the net, where it landed harmlessly between the legs of the prone Tanner St. John.

The crowd was silent.

The Fords hit the sand hard, rolling. Johnny saw Kevin grinning, his arms raised in victory. And it registered.

They won! They won!

Johnny screamed, and the crowd exploded.

Sixteen

CHAOS ERUPTED ALL around them. Spectators stormed the court. Sand flew up in all directions. Johnny hugged his brothers, hopping up and down and dancing and acting like they'd just won the championship of the universe.

"I can't believe we did it!" screamed Danny.

"I can!" hollered Kevin, his face smeared with sand. "I absolutely can!"

Then the girls were there. Raven with Danny. Penny with Kevin, wiping his face. And before Johnny could search for her, Kylie. At first they just stared at each other. Johnny was in shock. Should he hug her, should he kiss her, or should he just stand there and look stupid?

"Way to go, Johnny," she said, grinning.

Finally Johnny burst out laughing and grabbed Kylie, hugging the stuffing out of her. She hugged him right back, and Johnny felt the world falling away around him.

Penny's dad's voice roared over the microphone. It was time for the awards ceremony. A Fizz Cola representative handed over the big, fake, poster-board check for ten grand to the Fords. The poster board was big enough for all three of them to get their literally grubby hands on it. The trophy was amazing: three feet tall, a muscular dude holding a volleyball aloft. The engraving read: *The Inaugural Fizz Cola Surf City 3-on-3 Beach Volleyball Tournament Champions.* There was room below that for their names, which would be engraved later.

Tanner, Shooter, and Arliss showed up for their runner-up prizes. A check for a thousand bucks (made on a much smaller piece of poster board), a foot-tall trophy, and a Fizz Cola beach towel for each team member.

The ceremony broke up. Johnny gave the trophy to Danny and Kevin while he hung on to the check. He smiled and looked at it. It was what he'd wanted all along anyway. But knowing they won, knowing they beat the best team on the beach, was suddenly—and surprisingly, to Johnny—sweeter.

He sat on the edge of the dais, the first time he got to rest for hours. The big check was propped up next to him like a new friend. His eyes narrowed as he saw Tanner St. John approaching. Johnny prepared for the inevitable verbal confrontation, but he was too exhausted to even care what might come out of that garbage dump Tanner called a mouth.

But Tanner looked different—not his usual confident self. His hair was scraggly and full of sand. His face was drawn, his eyes dark. His shoulders slumped, carrying the weight of defeat. He held the little trophy in one hand and his Fizz beach towel in the other.

Johnny managed to stand. "Tanner."

Tanner nodded, but said nothing. He eyed Johnny with an unintelligible look. Hatred? Anger? Johnny couldn't tell.

"No hard feelings," Johnny finally said, extending his hand.

Tanner ignored the gesture. All he did was lean in and utter four curt words. "You're a player now."

With that, Tanner wrapped himself in his Fizz Cola beach towel, walked off the court, and disappeared. *Well, well*, Johnny thought, surprised. That was pretty decent of the guy.

Suddenly energized, he searched the crowd for Kylie but didn't see her anywhere. He spotted Kevin and Penny standing in a corner, talking with Danny and Raven. They were all grinning.

Johnny looked at his brothers, the knuckleheads who did so much to make his summer a living hell and then a raging success. Man, he loved them. They'd taught him a lot about himself and about life too. He waved at them, and they waved back. Kevin did a little dance, and Danny punched him on the arm.

Johnny laughed, then turned around, scanning the sea of people for Kylie.

There she was, standing under a palm tree, looking beautiful. But nervous.

"Hey, stranger," he said, walking toward her.

"Stranger by the minute," Kylie replied, her honey blond hair glistening in the sun. "I wasn't sure if I should stick around or not. I mean, if you wanted me to."

"You're not serious," he said.

"But you chose Jane. She was the one you wanted, not me."

"No, Kylie," he said, his eyes focused on hers. "I chose the *right thing* to do. The thing I've been doing my whole life. I didn't want to hurt Jane, and I didn't want to face the truth about my relationship with her. I was holding on to her like Excalibur."

Kylie tilted her head at him. She needed more, more assurance, something.

He would give it to her. "You know, when we were in trouble out there in the water yesterday afternoon, I saw Jane's face in my mind. And I thought that meant I loved her, that she was the one. But I realized afterward that I was wrong. A safety net and love are two different things. You tried to tell me that."

Kylie was gazing at him, her expression full of hope. "So what do we do now?"

"I have a really good idea," he said.

"What?" she asked.

He leaned over and kissed her on the lips, gently. Then he glanced up at her. "I think it's about time we did that."

"Oh, I think so too," she said, slipping her arms

around him. "In fact, how about we do it again?"

"Even better idea."

They kissed and kissed and kissed. A shiny new road was ahead of them, a road they'd travel together.

"It'll be really nice to know someone at Allman," Kylie teased, running her hands along his back and wrapping them around his shoulders.

"Definitely," Johnny replied, pulling her closer.

They stared into each other's eyes. As the surf pounded the beach, as the band on the dais kicked in to a new song, and as laughter and merriment swirled around them, Johnny kissed her again. A long, soft kiss.

It was the best thing Johnny did all day.

And it had been one amazing day. Not to mention one amazing summer.

"Hey, Johnny, Kylie," Kevin called.

They parted reluctantly from their kiss and glanced over.

"C'mon! Raven's bro is throwing a huge party for us at his house!"

Johnny smiled and grabbed Kylie's hand, and they ran laughing to meet his brothers and their girlfriends. And then the six of them walked away from the beach, much, much more than ten thousand dollars richer.

Do you ever wonder about falling in love? About members of the opposite sex? Do you need a little friendly advice but have no one to turn to? Well, that's where we come in . . . Jenny and Jake. Send us those questions you're dying to ask, and we'll give you the straight scoop on life and love.

DEAR JAKE

Q: *I really like my new boyfriend. The problem is that my ex-boyfriend is so jealous that he's trying to break us up by telling my new boyfriend lies about me. I'm afraid that my new boyfriend will start believing him. What should I do?*

HH, Westfield, MA

A: Tell your new boyfriend exactly what you told me. Everyone knows that jealous exes can't be believed, so I say you have zippo to worry about. But if he does start to believe the lies, well, then, he certainly doesn't trust you, does he? And then you'll have to have a whole different conversation with him.

Q: *I really like a guy at school, but I've never spoken to him. I've noticed him looking at me a few times. Does that mean he likes me?*

JM, Jamestown, NY

A: If you find him looking at you a lot, that means

he thinks you're cute or interesting and someone he'd probably like to meet. It's impossible to truly *like* anyone you've never actually spoken to.

DEAR JENNY

Q: *I have a huge crush on this boy. He seems very nice, but he's not that cute. I'm afraid that people will tease me for liking him, especially my best friend.*

RN, Sydney, Australia

A: I won't give you the standard "it's what *you* think that matters" since you already know that, *right?* So, I guess you'll just have to choose: (1) the *possibility* of getting teased by your friends—or (2) the *possibility* of going out with the guy you have a huge crush on. Hmmm. The first choice only gets you teased or not teased. The second choice might get you a date with your crush. Go for the guy you like. Even if your friends say, "I can't believe you like *him*," *you'll* still like him, and they'll still like you!

Q: *My friend is dating a guy I like. When I see them walking down the halls, holding hands, I feel just awful. What should I do?*

NG, Portland, OR

A: My heart goes out to you, big time. This is a really tough situation. Since the guy you like is taken—and by your friend, no less—he's definitely off-limits. And you can't exactly confide your feelings to your friend either. The good news is that a situation like this means you deserve at least three treats. Comfort yourself in little ways: a chocolate bar, a bubble bath, a new CD—whatever will make you smile. And soon enough you just might start to notice other guys. . . .

Do you have any questions about love?
Although we can't respond individually to your letters,
you just might find your questions answered in our column.

Write to:
Jenny Burgess or Jake Korman
c/o 17th Street Productions,
an Alloy Online, Inc. company.
33 West 17th Street
New York, NY 10011

Don't miss any of the books in *Love Stories*
—the romantic series from Bantam Books!

You'll always remember your first love.

Love Stories

Looking for signs he's ready to fall in love?

Want the guy's point of view?

Then you should check out *Love Stories*. Romantic stories that tell it like it is—why he doesn't call, how to ask him out, when to say good-bye.

Love Stories

Available wherever books are sold.